Deep:
A Twisted Tale of Deceptions

Deep:
A Twisted Tale of Deceptions

C. N. Phillips

www.urbanbooks.net

Urban Books, LLC
300 Farmingdale Road, NY-Route 109
Farmingdale, NY 11735

Deep: A Twisted Tale of Deceptions

ISBN 13: 978-1-62286-479-9
ISBN 10: 1-62286-479-4

First Trade Paperback Printing April 2017
Printed in the United States of America

10 9 8 7 6 5 4 3 2 1

Distributed by Kensington Publishing Corp.
Submit Orders to:
Customer Service
400 Hahn Road
Westminster, MD 21157-4627
Phone: 1-800-733-3000
Fax: 1-800-659-2436

Deep:
A Twisted Tale of Deceptions

by

C. N. Phillips

Prologue

"You can run, but you can't hide, Anna. I'm going to find youuuu!" an eerie voice rang out in the cold air.

Hearing the voice behind her made the panicked young woman run faster through the dimly lit concrete tunnel, feverishly checking behind her to make sure her stalker hadn't caught up to her. She had tears streaming down her face and her heart was pumping with terror, but she willed her legs to go as quickly as they could carry her. It was a task because whatever drug was still in her system was slowing her down and making the world around her a big blur. She cried out when she heard the voice taunting her because she knew the last place she wanted to be was in the clutches of her stalker.

"Please leave me alone!" she yelled behind her. "Just let me go!"

Dried blood coated her body, and the back of her once pretty, long, straight hair was matted. The more the drug wore off, the more she felt the pain from the open gashes crisscrossing her back.

"Anna," the voice echoed from a ways behind her, "you aren't going to make it out of here. Why are you running? Nobody leaves the Opulent Inn."

Anna sobbed uncontrollably but kept going. She didn't care that she was in shredded lingerie, or that she had black mascara running down her face, blurring her vision. She paid no attention to the fact that the skin on her body was sliced up to the point that it looked like she was fresh off the set of a gory horror movie where she, unfortunately, was the lead. She only had one objective: survival.

Finally she reached the end of the long hallway and fell into a tall wooden door. Feeling the rough shards of wood under her cheek, she used her shaky hands to grip the cold gold doorknob. She paused and tried to catch her breath. Knowing that she was lost underground somewhere, she just prayed that the door was unlocked and that the room she was about to enter had a window.

Twisting the knob, her heart leaped when it easily turned; and, without allowing another second to go to waste, she clambered through the open door. She glanced over her exposed brown shoulder and saw a shadow rounding a corner a ways away before she slammed the door shut behind her.

After she turned the lock on the doorknob she backed away from it slowly, trying to give her eyes time to adjust to the darkness of the room. The air was stuffy, making it hard for her to breathe, and the stench in there was almost unbearable; but she tried not to let that faze her.

"Window," she muttered to herself once she could see in the dark. "I need a window. Please, God, let me find a window."

On the floor there was a light that could only be given off by the moon, and Anna's insides fluttered with hope. She followed the light, ignoring the cold of the stone floor under her bare feet, until she finally found the source of the light. There was a window on the far wall and she saw that it was just big enough for her to get through it. Underneath it there was a box that she hurriedly stood on to reach what she hoped would be her salvation.

Anna extended her hand up and tried to unlatch the hook; but, for some reason, no matter how hard she tugged it wouldn't budge. Behind her she heard the doorknob begin to jiggle and her eyes darted toward the ground underneath the door. There was a shadow moving there and Anna began to sob. She was so close to evading her captor. All she had to do was open the window. She stood trembling on the tips of her toes so that she could get a better look at what she was doing. What she saw was enough to make her scream. There was a padlock on the other side of the window; there was no way to open it without a key.

"No!" she whimpered in disbelief. Balling her hand into a fist she tried to hit the window but she was far too weak to cause any real damage.

Anna stepped down from the box so that she could find something to bust through the glass with, but it was too late. The door was already wide open behind her and a sinister silhouette stood there holding a sharp machete that gleamed in the light. Anna knew there was nowhere to run, but still she was not ready to meet the fate staring her dead in the face. Defeated, Anna dropped to her knees and she wept.

"Please don't kill me," Anna begged through her sobs. "I don't want to die. Please don't kill me!"

Instead of responding, the silhouette walked slowly toward her, coming out of the shadows. Her figure was finally visible and the heels on her feet clicked with each step. When she finally reached Anna she knelt down and put her red lips next to the trembling young woman's ear.

"I told you not to run," she whispered into Anna's ear. "And you did."

"Please, Madame," Anna begged in a barely audible voice. "I don't want to die."

"If you don't want to die, then why would you run?" The woman put the cold metal of the machete against the nape of Anna's neck. "The only thing I asked from you was for you to be obedient, like the others, and in turn you disobeyed me. I could detach your head from your body and watch as your body twitched and your blood stained the floor . . . but I'm not going to."

"Y . . . you're not?"

"Of course not. Why would I kill you? You, my dear, have heart."

With quivering lips Anna looked up into the empty eyes of the person who had taken her entire life away. Freedom had been her desire for the past two weeks and she couldn't believe that she was going to be granted that. Maybe it had all been a test. A sick test.

"Y . . . you're going to let me go?" Anna breathed.

"I said I'm not going to kill you," the woman said and chuckled at the naïveté of the girl before her. She gently gripped the bottom of Anna's chin and stared coldheartedly into her eyes. "But you will never be free. You belong to me. And this?" The woman motioned to the machete and placed it in Anna's hand before standing. "That is yours. Follow me. You have work to do."

Chapter 1

"Stop looking back!" a voice yelled into the night air. "And keep up before you get hit!"

The sound of automatic rounds being fired plagued the night air as two thieves ran for their lives. Both were dressed in all black and had a duffle bag on their shoulders. Hearts pounding violently, they kept their hooded heads ducked down as they pushed their feet to go as fast as they could. Bullets ricocheted off of the concrete and found homes in the cars parked on the street of the neighborhood they were running through. The neighborhood they were in was lit up by the streetlights, and people were peeking through their windows to see what all the commotion was outside of their homes.

"Move! Move!" one of the thieves shouted to a young woman who appeared out of nowhere. She had just stepped out of her white Toyota Corolla clutching a bag of groceries in her hand. She stood like a deer caught in a pair of headlights as she watched the two people running her way, waving wildly at her to move.

The warning came too late; she didn't even see her death coming. She was clipped by multiple bullets in the center of her chest and blasted backward off of her feet. Her body slid down her car, smearing blood on the white paint the whole way down, and her eyes would forever be frozen open in surprise until somebody closed them.

There was no time to be sad at the innocent life lost because the assailants running after them weren't letting up. The thieves were forced to make a quick right turn through somebody's open gate and run on their neatly trimmed yard. The two lucked out because the backyard of the house led straight into the alley where they had parked their getaway vehicle. The first thief dropped the duffle bag onto the ground while still running full speed in front of the second. Jumping the fence effortlessly the thief waited for the partner to throw both duffle bags over before following suit. Once they were both over they picked the bags back up and continued their pace toward where the 2010 all-black Chevy Tahoe was parked in the shadows.

"They're getting close!" the first thief said, jumping on and sliding over the hood of the truck.

"Hurry up and start the truck then!" the second thief yelled, yanking open the passenger's door and hopping in before slamming it shut.

Looking to the right they saw the young thugs still toting their automatic weapons and climbing the fence.

"Go! Go!" the second thief said, and ducked just in time because the thugs wasted no time unloading their bullets into the vehicle.

The windows on the right side of the truck were instantly shattered and the first thief ducked down in the driver's seat. The rapid fire made it almost impossible to sit back up, but with still hands the thief turned the key and started the engine. Driving was slightly hard due to the fact that both of their heads were ducked and neither could see, but the driver was adamant about getting them out of there. Turning the steering wheel all the way left, the driver hit a U-turn and mashed on the gas. With a loud screech they made a swift getaway before their opponents were able to get too close to them. They kept their heads down until they were sure they were out of range of the guns shooting at them.

"Hit that right." The thief in the passenger's seat guided the driver with expertise through North Omaha. "I parked off of Twenty-fourth and Lake by where the Blue Lion used to be, so take the back streets."

"Why would you park so far from the job?"

"So if they followed us it would give us more time to lose them. Just shut up and drive, dude. You always have something to say."

The tension in the car wasn't uncommon after a job that led to a near-death experience for the pair. They didn't head in the direction of where the second car was parked until they were certain they weren't being followed. Once they got as close as they needed to, they parked the shot-up truck in front of an abandoned house and wiped down the inside of it before grabbing the two duffle bags. It wasn't the first time the two had ditched a car so they both knew the drill; nothing was left behind. Shielded by the night sky, they ran the remaining two blocks to the gold 2002 Chevy Impala they had stolen earlier that day.

"What time is it?"

"Almost ten," the second thief said, pulling away from the curb and finally removing the face mask. "Take your mask and hoodie off so we can dump them on the way home."

"Sometimes I swear you're the big sister and not me, Rhonnie."

Rhonnie smirked at her older sister as she drove up Lake Street. "You know I've always been the more responsible one. Two years means nothing, Ahli."

"Sike. Just get us home. Turn on some Eric Bellinger. His voice always calms me down after a night like this."

Rhonnie did as she was told and turned on her sister's favorite song by Eric: "Imagination." Although she wanted to discuss the contents of the bags they had in the back seat, she knew it wasn't the time or the place. She knew that their father had sent them on the mission for a reason; but usually they robbed people of cash and jewels, sometimes artwork. *Not—*

"Stop thinking so much," Ahli interrupted Rhonnie's thoughts with her head laid back and her eyes closed. She already knew what was going on through her sister's nosey head. "I want to know too, but we can ask him when we get home."

As always, Ahli was reading her mind. Sometimes Rhonnie felt like the two of them should have been twins by the way they were always in sync. Rhonnie couldn't do anything but sigh and continue driving. She was trying to get back out West as fast as she could because she knew their current area would soon be swarming with cops and that was the last thing that they needed. They rode, listening to the soft crooning coming from the speakers for the next thirty minutes, until they finally reached their destination.

Pressing the circular button on the remote hanging from the Impala's visor, Rhonnie pulled the car into the garage of the vast five-bedroom brick house. She planned to dump the car early the next day; however, at that moment, they needed to sit still for a while. The streets were too hot for them to be anywhere but home right then, especially since they knew for sure at least one person got killed.

The girls grabbed the bags from the back seat of the car and walked inside of the house, but not before shutting the garage door behind them.

"Dad!" Rhonnie yelled out, not able to contain herself. She didn't care if he was asleep. "Daddy!"

"Chill, NaNa," Ahli said, shooting her little sister a look as they made their way into the living room of their home.

"Fuck that," Rhonnie said, dropping the bag she was holding on the coffee table. She plopped down on the black leather couch. After she kicked the black Timberlands off of her feet she crossed her arms and shook her foot impatiently.

Her eyes were focused on the spiral staircase by the foyer of the house, and they stayed there until she saw the familiar Ralph Lauren house slippers making their way down the carpeted steps. When Quinton Malone entered the living room a smile spread on his face as soon as he saw both of the duffle bags on the black marble coffee table.

"Good work," he told them; but his smile soon faded when his eyes met his younger daughter's. "Why the long face, NaNa?"

Rhonnie took a deep breath before she mustered up the courage to come at her father with any form of disrespect. She glanced at Ahli, who in turn just shrugged her shoulders.

So much for backup, Rhonnie thought. "Daddy, why you got us stealing coke?" she finally asked. "You had us getting shot at for cocaine! Of all things! Since when did you become a drug dealer?"

Quinton figured that the question would be coming so he was prepared for it. He sat down in his favorite chair, the La-Z-Boy diagonal from the couch that his daughters were sitting on. He observed them and saw the sweat still glistening on their foreheads and the tiredness in their eyes. He felt a small pang of guilt, but not enough to regret sending them to do the job. It wasn't the first time that they had been shot at, and he was sure that it wouldn't be the last either. He stared his daughter square in the eyes until she blinked.

"I never said I was a drug dealer." He spoke in a smooth voice, but his children knew him well enough to recognize the deadly undertone. "The contents in those bags are probably only worth fifty thousand dollars combined. I have a buyer who is willing to pay double that."

"Sounds a lot like drug dealing," Rhonnie said, raising her eyebrow. Although the last thing she wanted to do was go against him, she had to let him know that she didn't agree with him. "If you would have told us what we were really jacking I would have never gone."

"Exactly the reason I didn't say anything. I need you both to trust me."

"Trust you? I do trust you but, Daddy, having that in the house is probably the dumbest thing we have ever done. I don't want to be around it. Period. And you had us out there risking our lives for it. I thought we were there to grab bags of money. This was supposed to be one of our last jobs."

"That is money, or it will be. This is an opportunity that I can't pass up. Can you?"

"If I would have known I was going to be robbing a house full of people with automatic weapons I definitely would have," Rhonnie shot back, not letting up on her dad.

Quinton sighed and rubbed his large hand down the neatly trimmed beard on his face. Whereas Ahli was more like their mother, Rhonnie was just like him. From her bullheaded frame of mind to her stubborn attitude, she was definitely Quinton Jr. However, he knew she had a "get money" mentality just like him, so that was what he homed in on at that moment.

"So, you're going to let the job you just did go unpaid for? A'ight, go drop those bags off somewhere then, miss out on all of that money. I'll hit Lance up and see if has another job for you."

For that, Rhonnie had no comment. She had become accustomed to being able to drive any kind of car she wanted and being able to wear whatever designer she saw fit. Instead of responding to her father she just looked at her feet. Inside she was fuming but, he was right, she didn't just risk her life for nothing.

"When do they expect us to deliver?" Ahli finally chimed in. "Because, Rhonnie is right, we need to get that stuff out of the house as soon as possible, Daddy. I don't feel right being around it. I know we do some bad shit, but we ain't never had to lay a hand on narcotics. If this is the first time, it has to be the last time."

She stared into her father's warm face and noticed that he must have gotten his brush cut lined up and his beard trimmed while they were out handling business earlier that day. He was looking debonair and sophisticated even in his clean night clothes. It didn't bother her that he primped himself while they were out putting in work; it pleased her that he wasn't worried about them. It showed the faith that he had in their skills. What bothered her was that he'd kept the contents of what they were stealing a secret.

"In two days," Quinton told her, clasping his hands together. "The drop happens at one o'clock on Friday. In Miami."

"Miami!" Rhonnie exclaimed. "That drive is like twenty-four hours!"

"Twenty-three," Quinton corrected her. "And that's the reason why we need to rest up, because we are leaving first thing in the morning."

Ahli wanted the drugs gone, but she didn't say that she wanted to move it *that* soon. The two girls would barely have enough time to recuperate from the job they had just done before they would be on another one. Still, she knew better than to argue with her father. She had more respect for him than that. Rhonnie, on the other hand, just couldn't seem to contain her thoughts.

"Tomorrow? How does Uncle Lance even know these people are good for their word?" Rhonnie asked skeptically.

"Because your Uncle Lance has never steered me wrong. Ever." Quinton winked at Rhonnie. "Now shut up and listen."

Both Rhonnie and Ahli got quiet, knowing that their father was about to brief them on how things would go the next day. He usually didn't go on jobs, but he felt like he had no choice but to be present for the one at hand. He explained to them that they would take two cars and leave thirty minutes apart. He told them that the drugs would be hidden in the car with them, just to stay on the safe side of things. Quinton knew he had eyes on him because he wasn't supposed to leave the state; however, he knew his parole officer, Beverly, would let him slide. Still, the last thing he needed was to get pulled over with two bags of bricks in his vehicle.

Risky as it seemed he knew, as long as Ahli drove, the girls would be all right. He already booked them separate rooms at the Hilton. When they got there they were to park in the back of the hotel and check in like normal, but leave the duffle bags of drugs in the car. Afterward, they were to shower and stay in their room until he called them.

"Sounds easy enough," Ahli said, nodding, seemingly pleased with the plan.

"They always seem easy," Rhonnie said, standing and stretching her arms wide. "But are they ever easy? No. I'm going to bed since we have to be back up in like six hours. Night, y'all." She didn't wait for them to say it back before she made her exit.

Quinton sighed and shook his head. "That girl doesn't know how badly I want to ring her neck sometimes," he said aloud and mostly to himself.

"She's just young, Daddy," Ahli said. "She loves the money, but sometimes I think she had to grow up too fast."

"Yeah." He sighed, rubbing his hands together. "I never wanted this for you girls. It just seemed like the only way back then."

"I know, Daddy." Ahli shrugged her shoulders. "But it's just what we have to do for now. Nobody knew Mommy was going to die or that we would have to struggle the way that we were. That's not your fault and I understand why you brought us into your world. And until you get right, I don't mind going in your place."

Quinton smiled at his oldest daughter. She was a compelling young woman, just like her mother had been. He admired the fact that she wasn't scared to get her hands dirty to feed her family. When it came to Rhonnie or him, she turned into an untamed beast. He'd seen firsthand what her aim could do to the opposition. She was a natural when it came to gunplay, and she was an asset to his little team of thieves.

"I know you understand the game, LaLa, but try to tell all that to your sister."

"She's still a kid living the life of an adult," Ahli told him. "She wants to enjoy her youth, and it seems like time is winding down. I keep telling her just a couple more jobs and we won't have to do this anymore. Give her a couple of days. Once she sees all that money she'll be all right."

She stood up and planted a kiss on Quinton's forehead before she too bounded up the stairs, leaving him lost in his thoughts.

***

"Sister, wake up." An impatient voice invaded Rhonnie's dreams.

She groaned, trying to roll over and bury her body deeper into her lavender fleece cover. It literally felt like she had just closed her eyes and that sleep hadn't even found her yet. All she wanted was to stay lost behind her eyelids and forget about what needed to be done once she opened them. "Fihh muh minutes," she mumbled into her soft pillow.

"No!" she heard a stern voice say; and then she felt the covers being yanked off of her. "It's already five thirty in the morning. Get up! I'm trying to get this shit done and over with."

"Ahli!" Rhonnie yelled as the gust of cold air hit her bare legs. Her eyes popped open and sure enough there was her big sister standing in front of her, wide awake. Ahli was fully dressed in a form-fitting T-shirt and a pair of Levi skinny jeans that hugged her hips and made her thighs look extra thick. Rhonnie was forced to squint her eyes because the light was too bright in the room. "What is wrong with you? I'm sleepy, sister!"

"Sleep in the car," Ahli responded and threw some clothes at her little sister.

Thursday morning had come faster than Rhonnie had anticipated, and getting out of her comfortable bed felt like torture. Rhonnie looked up at her sister again and took in her appearance. Her kinky, long, curly hair was pulled back into a neat ponytail, her mocha skin was clear and smooth, and her eyelashes were long and smooth as if she had put mascara on them. It was apparent that her sister had been up for a while.

"Fuck," she mumbled to herself and sat up, stretching her arms out. Her eyelids were still heavy but she knew with Ahli hovering over her there would be no going back to sleep. The smell of food cooking invaded her nostrils and her mouth instantly began to water. "Is Daddy up?"

"Yeah, he's downstairs," Ahli said. "He made breakfast for us and he said he has one more thing to tell us before we leave. I already packed your bag so don't worry about it. Fucking with you we wouldn't leave until noon."

Rhonnie grinned sheepishly before she stood up from her bed and stumbled slightly. Using her knuckles she wiped her eyes, trying to force herself to wake up. "Okay. I'll meet you downstairs. Let me get in the shower."

"I'm giving you twenty minutes tops." Ahli gave her little sister a knowing look. "If I have to come back up here and get you, it's problems."

"Okay, Mother."

When Ahli left the room Rhonnie grabbed the clothes that were thrown at her: a simple pair of jeans, a cotton Ralph Lauren T-shirt, a pair of boy-short panties with the purchase tag still attached, and a pair of socks. Rhonnie smiled to herself. Although Ahli was only two years older she had really stepped up to the motherly role when their mother died. Ahli was so busy being strong for everybody else that Rhonnie knew that it would be messed up to ever give her a hard time about anything. So most times she listened to her sister because her judgment was usually right. Rhonnie couldn't count on one hand anymore how many bullets should have entered her body if it weren't for her big sister looking out for her.

She made her way to the bathroom in her bedroom so she could prepare for the day. For ten minutes she stood in the shower, relishing the feeling of the hot water smacking her body. Once she was done she dried off, applied her favorite lotion, and then attempted to do something with her long, thick hair. When all else failed she ended up simply mimicking the ponytail that her sister was wearing, but swooping her edges more neatly than Ahli had. Once finished she studied herself in the mirror until she was satisfied with her appearance.

"I'm cute as hell," she said, realizing how vain she sounded; but she didn't care. She was the perfect blend of her mother and her father. She had her mother's doe-like chestnut brown eyes, sharp cheekbones, and smooth caramel skin. From her father she got his curly grade of hair, full lips, and his smile.

Knowing that she was about to go over the time limit that Ahli had given her, she hurried out of her room and down the stairs toward the kitchen. She heard her dad going over the events of the next day with Ahli once more, and when he saw her enter the kitchen he motioned for her to take a seat next to her sister. There was already a plate in front of the chair he was directing her to. Noticing that their plates were scraped clean she knew they must have eaten while she was still getting ready; she didn't care, though. She was just happy her food was still hot. Honestly, even if it were cold she would still eat it. Her dad threw down in the kitchen.

"Good morning, Daddy," Rhonnie said, kissing him on his forehead. She smirked at his comfortable travel outfit. Even though he was dressed down in a Nike jogging suit with all-white Nike Roshes, he was fly. She still was upset at him for what he had done, but after a good night's sleep she realized that the damage was already in the wind.

"When we leaving?" she asked after she was seated.

"Right after you eat."

"Okay," she said, stuffing her mouth with food. She chewed and swallowed a big bite before turning to her sister. "Why were you up so early? I was tired as hell after last night."

"I know, Big Hungry," Ahli said, reaching out and brushing a bacon crumb from her lip. "That's why I took the initiative to get up and dump that Impala we were in last night."

Rhonnie grinned before dousing her scrambled eggs with Louisiana hot sauce and taking a big bite. "Thanks, sister."

"Uh-huh."

Quinton waited patiently for Rhonnie to finish her food before he took the two slightly weighted black boxes from his lap and placed them on the wooden kitchen table. He saw their eyes light up the way they always did when he bought them gifts, and he slid a box in front of each of them. "Go ahead, open them."

Ahli and Rhonnie snatched the tops off of their boxes at the same time. When they saw the contents of the boxes they didn't know whether to be excited or skeptical. Rhonnie took hers out and eyed the black Ruger LC9 in her hand. Ahli did the same with her Ruger SR45 and they both looked back up at their father in wonder after a few moments.

"It was time that you got new ones," was all he said before he stood up and grabbed their empty plates. "Since you two always want to wear those tight-ass jeans, those are compact enough to fit in your purses. Brand new as well; no bodies can be connected to them."

"No bodies can be connected to any of my guns," Rhonnie said matter-of-factly.

Ahli snickered before she glanced at the clock on the wall. Seeing that it was time to handle business, she stood and waved for Rhonnie to follow. "Come on, NaNa." She motioned to her sister. "It's time to get this show on the road."

Rhonnie was still eyeing her new toy and she shook her head incredulously. "Great. We're traveling across the world with drugs and guns. Just great."

Chapter 2

Somebody real is hard to find
Somebody worth all your time
Somebody who can tell you the truth
Someone who loves you for you.

Tink's voice blessed the inside of the 2015 Chevy Camaro with a beautiful melody. The fact that she would be in a car literally all day didn't sit well with Ahli, but having good music to keep her time occupied made it better. She also thought about all of the money that they would be bringing home and that eased her mind a little bit. Although she was only twenty-one years old she had grown accustomed to her life by now.

After their mother died when she was thirteen and Rhonnie was eleven she watched her father suffer the worst depression ever in front of them. He tried to hide it, but she read through all of his fake smiles. He struggled to find a job simply because nobody wanted to hire a convicted felon and there were times that he didn't have enough money to feed them all, so he would go without a meal for days. It was hard for Ahli to watch that, but whenever she would try and force him to eat some of her food he would refuse. "Everything I do, I do it for you girls. To put and keep food in your mouths. I made a promise to your mother and I plan on keeping it. As long as I am able to do that, I am fed." He would say that over and over until eventually Ahli acquired that mindset as well.

At age thirteen Ahli understood things that other kids her age didn't. Their mother was gone and that meant her money was, too. She learned that since her parents had never been legally wed her father had no claim to whatever money she had in her accounts. Technically the money should have gone to her children, but it never did. Quinton tried to hire a lawyer to fight for the money and assets but eventually he just gave up. He was spending too much money and time jumping through hoops for a prize that wasn't even guaranteed. They were used to living in a house and riding in nice vehicles, and went to suddenly living in a one-bedroom apartment and repeating clothes in the same week.

Ahli mourned their mother for a long time. She wasn't the same kid after. She and Rhebecca had been very close so it was hard to come to terms with the fact that she would never see her again. Although Ahli wanted to sit around and mope she knew she couldn't. One day she would be the woman Rhonnie would have to look up to so she figured she'd step into those shoes early. Any sadness she felt from their mother's death she began to keep hidden. To her the little bit of money that her father got she felt shouldn't have to go to food because she wanted him to focus on bills and she would focus on the meals. She was too young to get a job so she didn't have a choice; she had to steal it.

Anything to keep food in Rhonnie's mouth, she always told herself before she went into any grocery store. She would wear baggy clothes so that she could carry her trophies out without them falling to the ground. She would often go around the first week of the month since she knew it would be packed full of people using their welfare checks. There must have been a special kind of angel watching over her because, over the years, before they started really getting money, she never got caught once. Just as she started reflecting on the day that truly started their reign, Rhonnie interrupted her thoughts.

"Do you think everything will be okay?"

Ahli was quiet at first. The question her sister had just asked was one she'd been playing over and over inside of her own head since the moment they pulled away from the house. She pursed her lips to stop herself from being too blunt. She knew that her sister always based her own emotions off of her big sister. Which was why Ahli couldn't let on that she was feeling skeptical.

"I don't think Uncle Lance would put us into a harmful situation," she finally answered.

"But Daddy doesn't even know these people. A couple of phone calls doesn't mean anything."

"Daddy trusts the situation. We will be fine."

"Daddy bought us new guns, LaLa. He don't trust shit."

To that Ahli had no response, simply because she had been thinking the same thing.

"Thanks for making me feel better about it," Rhonnie said sarcastically when her sister had no rebuttal. "Thanks so much."

Ahli smirked over at her sister who sat in the tan leather passenger's seat of the gold 2015 Camaro she'd just purchased herself. Rhonnie sighed deeply and folded her arms across her chest like a big baby.

"You scared?" Ahli teased.

"Sike!" Rhonnie scoffed.

"So what you acting like that for then? You act like this is the first job that you've ever been on."

"I didn't say that . . . but this is the last one."

"What?" Ahli took her eyes off of the road one more time to look at the serious expression on Rhonnie's face. Her jaw line was visible and it was apparent that she was clenching her teeth together.

"You heard me," Rhonnie said, looking straight ahead. "I'm done after this. I'm tired of it all. I want to enjoy my youth. I want to be normal."

"Well, newsflash, little bitch, you're not normal. We're not normal. You can't be normal with your body count."

"That's part of the job. I killed them because I had to."

"And why did you have to?"

"Because they were trying to kill me first!"

"Exactly," Ahli said, grabbing her smartphone and changing the song playing through the aux cord. "How many normal people do you know who have people trying to kill them?"

It was Rhonnie's turn to be silent. Instead she pulled over her head the hood of the red Nebraska hoodie that she'd thrown on before she'd left. She reached and changed the song, not wanting to hear any soft lyrics any longer. Slouching down in her seat she placed her forehead on the cold window and allowed herself to get lost in Don Trip's voice and lyrics.

Quinton drove five miles behind his daughters with no doubt in his mind that they would be all right. Hearing about the obstacles they had to overcome to get the product they were driving with would have scared any other father, but not him. He was proud. It proved to him that his daughters could handle anything and it also proved that he had trained them right.

Sometimes he felt guilty for introducing them to the lifestyle, but he knew that they had no other choice that was better. After Rhebecca died he was flat broke. Even the money that they had gotten together was in her bank account and he had no claim to it since the two were never legally married. Being a convicted felon for armed burglary, it was impossible for him to get a job that would take care of the three of them. With the girls being so young at the time he didn't want to risk going to jail again and getting locked away forever, so for a while he just sucked it up. He worked odd jobs, pretty much anything to keep a roof over their heads. But the girls were getting older, their needs were becoming more expensive, and he could barely keep up. At that point in time he felt like less of a man, but his girls always seemed to make him feel as though he was a superhero. He drove, rubbing his facial hair, and reflected on the day that changed their lives.

Quinton flexed his muscles right before he reached out and opened the door to his parole officer's office. He would have rather been anywhere but there, but he knew it was a term of his early release; and, for the sake of his daughters, he would abide by the rules. Still, he was agitated because all he could think about were all of the things his kids needed. Rhonnie's jeans were too short and Ahli needed some new tennis shoes before hers fell all the way apart. It hurt his heart to be living the way that they were, but he was doing the best that he could. He couldn't move the way that he wanted to in the streets, no matter how much his hands itched because they needed to be put to work. He was on papers still and the last thing he wanted was to be sent back to prison and have his kids in foster care.

"On time as usual I see, Quinton," Quinton's parole officer, Beverly Nichols, said when she saw him.

"Yeah," Quinton said, walking up to her desk. He grabbed the cup that had his initials on it. "Just tryin'a get this done and over with so I can go home."

"I see," Beverly said, standing up from her desk and eyeing the handsome man. She always looked forward to her monthly meeting with him because he was the only man who made her blood boil. It turned her on to

see him walk in there in his Ralph Lauren getup, but it turned her on even more to hear his deep baritone voice speak.

Although he had done some questionable things to get him to where he was then, it didn't take from the knowledge that was embedded in his head. Whenever she spoke to him she felt like a student and, to her, he was so sexy because of his intellect. The only thing stopping her from letting him bend her over her desk was the fact that she needed her job; still, she knew it would happen one day. She walked Quinton to the bathroom and waved him inside. She stood in the doorway and, as usual, waited for him to do his thing.

Quinton felt Beverly's presence behind him as he whipped his monster out so that he could do what he came to do. The sound of him urinating filled the office bathroom and he looked over his shoulder at Beverly and saw that her eyes were glued to his third leg. He smirked to himself, shaking his head. Beverly was a beautiful woman with a nice, shapely body, but to him she had nothing on Rhebecca. Honestly, in his mind, nobody did.

When he was done he zipped his pants back up and screwed the top on the bottle. After setting it down on the sink next to the toilet he washed his hands.

"There you go," he said, walking out of the bathroom and nodding toward the sink. "Anything else you need from me?"

Your dick inside of me, *Beverly wanted to say, but instead she offered up a kind smile and motioned for him to take a seat at her desk with her. She sat in her big, comfy black rolling chair while he sat in a stiff, wooden one opposite her. He placed his hands on his knees versus her desk and watched her thumb through the folder that was in front of her.*

"Hmmm," she said, eyeing the paperwork in her hands.

Quinton impatiently tapped his foot and checked the clock on the wall. It was almost three o'clock and he knew that the school bus would be dropping the girls off soon. He didn't like for them to be home alone in the neighborhood they lived in, so he was hoping that Beverly would hurry the meeting up.

"It says here that you don't have any kids. When are you going to settle down and have some children, Quinton?"

Beverly's question caught him off guard. He looked at her like she was crazy. "What? I d—" he started so say.

"A fine man like you would make some beautiful babies," she interrupted him. "Settle down, get married. Despite your bad choices you seem like a good man."

"Can I . . ." Quinton motioned toward the paperwork. "Can I see those for a second?"

Beverly handed him the paperwork and he glimpsed over it. Sure enough his file stated that he was a thirty-seven-year-old single man with a felony for burglary. Nowhere in the paperwork did it say that he had children. His brow furrowed a bit as he tried to make sense of it; but after a few seconds it hit him.

"Rhebecca," he said in a voice so low that only he could hear it.

It slipped his mind that Rhebecca never allowed him to sign the girl's birth certificates. And although they were under his name at the school they went to, that never got reported back to the law, since legally paternity was never proven for either of them. He and Rhebecca both agreed that it was the best way to protect them from their pasts. He handed Beverly the file back and shrugged his shoulders casually.

"I don't know." He smiled to himself, standing. "I don't know what kid would be able to handle me as a father. Are we done for the day? I have to get going."

"You're always in a rush to get up out of here." Beverly winked at him. "I don't bite."

"But I do," he said, heading toward the door. "Have a good day, Beverly."

Walking out of her office he went straight toward his 1997 Crown Vic. He thought about his oldest daughter. She thought that he didn't know that she was robbing the grocery stores blind just to put food in the house. He also thought about Rhonnie. She thought that he didn't know about her picking pockets just so that she could slide an extra twenty in his wallet for gas.

Things had been so hard on them since Rhebecca died, and he gripped the steering wheel tightly as he drove up Fifty-sixth Street just thinking about it. This wasn't the life that they wanted to give their girls, nor was it the life that he promised to give them. Him not knowing whether he was going to get or keep a job or be able to even put dinner on the table that night. Them having to be subjected to a life of struggle when they used to never have to worry about a thing. He promised Rhebecca on her deathbed that he would take care of them by any means necessary. It was finally time to show and prove.

In Quinton's day, when Ahli was a baby and Rhonnie wasn't even thought about, he was what they called the "Lick Man." It started when he and Rhebecca first got together under unruly circumstances. They ran away together with nothing but themselves and a baby in tow. He had to feed his family somehow. Being the Lick Man, he was the person called for high-priced armed robberies, whether it was for material posses-sion or just information. His body count was high due to the precision of his aim and because he always got the job done. He never kept anything from the places he robbed; he was a hired hand and collected his fee prior to every job. For years his jobs were precise; however, he messed up the last hit he ever did alone.

The job was to break into a lawyer's house and get all the files on the case he was working on against the man who had hired Quinton. His calculations on the house were all wrong. He didn't expect the housekeeper to be there and he hesitated at pulling the trigger. His eyes had gone to her round, pregnant belly and she reminded him immensely of the family he had at home. That split second of hesitation cost him everything because she was able to run off and call the police. They caught him a few blocks away. Although the judge couldn't connect him with any prior robberies he was still sentenced to ten years. He was blessed to see the birth of Rhonnie before they took him away.

He knew that he couldn't move the way he wanted to, especially since they let him out after only doing five years and he was still on probation. For six years after his release he and his family lived the American Dream. They had the house in the suburbs of Nebraska, the cars, and even the white picket fence. Rhebecca was a woman who held him down, but when she died he realized they couldn't afford living the way that they were. It wasn't right.

He stroked his facial hair and nodded. He sighed and at that moment he made a decision. Pulling out his phone he dialed a number and as the phone rang he held his breath.

"Hello?" a familiar voice said on the other end.

Lance McGee was Quinton's oldest friend, and also the person who aligned him with everyone he had done jobs for in the past.

"I'm ready," Quinton stated simply.

"Got tired of mopping them floors, huh?" Lance chuckled into the phone. "Well, let's get this set then. I'll text you an address where we can meet and talk in person."

"Okay," Quinton said. "But it won't just be me. I have a new proposition for you."

Lance paused again on the other end, as if he pondered Quinton's words. "All right," he said finally. "Be looking out for my text."

"Bet. One." Quinton disconnected the phone and tossed it in the passenger's seat.

Just because he couldn't move like he used to didn't mean that they couldn't. He was going to teach Rhonnie and Ahli everything he knew about armed robbery. And, that time around, they would keep everything.

That night when he went home he sat both of his daughters down and told them the complete truth about who he was and why he was locked up for five years of their lives. He explained to them that their "uncle Lance" was not really their uncle and that they had once done gritty business together. He told them that when they were living well in the big house out West, it was because he was a high-paid burglar and their mother had money saved up. After he got released from prison too many eyes were on him, so he couldn't get money like he used to . . . but they could.

"So you want us to rob people?"

"Yes," Quinton answered Ahli bluntly. "But not just anybody. The rich, and you will give to the poor: yourselves. You deserve the world, don't you? Sometimes the only way to get it is to take it. You will be hired hands, your uncle Lance will set up the jobs, and your hits will be calculated. You will have to be trained."

"Will you teach us?"

From where he sat across from them he studied their faces. Their expressions reflected that of an undying allegiance. He couldn't fail them. All he wanted to do was provide for them. He would do anything for them to be happy, except the one thing that would take him from them for the rest of his life. Instead, he would show them how to be better than him. They had no records and, if he could help it, they would never get caught.

"Of course. Everything I know so that you can learn from my mistakes. A few jobs to get us on our feet and we're out. If you ever want to stop, we're out."

"What about Beverly?" Ahli asked him. "Won't she be suspicious if she suddenly sees you with a lot of money?"

"I will continue to work odd jobs to keep eyes from lingering on us longer than they should. You won't have to worry about me. But I need the two of you to understand this world is very dangerous. There is nothing fun about it and it can be a deadly game."

"I saw a crackhead get murdered last week by her supposed friend," Rhonnie said under her breath. "And a group of gang members shoot some kid in the neck the next day. Just by living here we are already part of a deadly game."

Rhonnie and Ahli looked at each other first and then around at their shabby, tiny apartment. Tears came to Rhonnie's eyes and she took her sister's hand.

"I don't want to live like this anymore, LaLa. I want life to go back to how it was when Mom was alive. If we stay here it could be us out in the street bleeding out because of a stray bullet."

Ahli hugged her sister close and then looked back to her father with certainty in her eyes.

"Okay. We're in, Daddy."

The rest was history. Quinton snapped out of his flashback and smirked to himself. He had indeed taught his daughters everything he knew and they had developed a few of their own tricks. They were anyone's best shooters' worst nightmare, and unlike him they never messed up on a job. He trained them for a whole summer before he let them go on their first job. He taught them how to fight and he also taught them how to shoot with precision.

The thing about his daughters that saddened him the most with it all was that they never once questioned him or acted afraid. The times had hardened their hearts, and their surroundings made it no better. The one-bedroom apartment they lived in was in a bad neighborhood in North Omaha. The things they saw were things no teenager should have ever seen. Ahli should have been preparing to go off to college and Rhonnie should have been preparing for the ACT; but their reality consumed them, and the only thing that mattered was survival.

Checking the clock in his car he saw that he had a little over ten hours left to go in the drive. Placing his sunglasses over his eyes he leaned back in his leather seat and steered with one hand. He trusted Lance and was eager to get the drop over with. The only thing on his mind was the money, no matter the cost.

They drove the next ten hours straight through and only stopped for gas or food. Once they got to the hotel Rhonnie and Ahli were beyond tired. Quinton didn't want to be in town longer than needed, so both girls wanted to capitalize off of what might have been their one and only opportunity to sleep. They could vacation and sightsee at a later date.

The time read six thirty in the morning and both girls dropped their bags at the door of the hotel room. Exhausted, they fell onto one of the queen-sized beds in the spacious room. Ahli lay on her back with her head resting on one of the fluffy pillows, while Rhonnie sprawled out across the bed with her head on Ahli's stomach.

"Should we go get that from the car?" She yawned and stretched out.

"No," Ahli said matter-of-factly. "Nobody knows it's there and if somebody tries to break into the car I'll get a notification to my phone. Plus, Daddy said leave it in the car."

Rhonnie rolled her eyes at her sister. Ahli was always downloading new apps to her phone that nobody else would even think to download. "Okay, phone wiz, just make sure your sound is on so that we don't miss Daddy's call. Knowing him he ain't even coming straight to the hotel anyway."

"I'm already knowing. I'm just going to set my alarm for us to wake up in two hours. By then I'm sure he'll be ready for the drop."

"And then back on the road we go," Rhonnie mumbled sleepily. Her eyes were already closed and she put her arm over her face.

"With all that money," Ahli said and smiled before she too closed her eyes and succumbed to a much-needed slumber.

Chapter 3

Quinton knew his daughters like the back of his hand. He was positive that neither was currently waiting for his phone call. He could bet his life that both of them were passed out in the same bed catching some much-needed Z's. He hadn't planned on going directly to the hotel anyway so he didn't mind too much, as long as they were ready when he called.

Instead of going to the hotel and catching up on his own sleep Quinton decided to go scope out the area that he would be at with his daughters in some hours. Not because he didn't trust Lance's connections, but because he was a man to never go into a situation blind. The last thing he wanted to do was lead his only children into an ambush.

He drove toward the address in Overtown that Lance had given him, only to find out that he couldn't turn down the street that he needed because it was completely blocked off. Lance had warned Quinton over the phone that the whole neighborhood was its own city. The king of the hood, Dot, didn't take too kindly to strangers. He was as ruthless as they came and an invite was required to get into the neighborhood. If you were not expected then there would be no questioning; you would die on sight.

Quinton, of course, then questioned what Dot's hold on the law was. Certainly the police were constantly patrolling the area to scope out any wrongdoing, but evidently he was wrong. Dot had the law sewn up to the point where they didn't even look his way if they didn't have to. Lance told him that any detective who had come after Dot was on the memorial wall at the station, and because of that he was allowed to do business in peace. That right there let Quinton know what kind of man he was dealing with, and it was exactly the reason why he had to come and scope out the surroundings.

To the normal eye it just seemed like the street was having some construction done to it, but Quinton's eyes trained on something the average eye wouldn't. He drove as close as he could to the roadwork so that he could see past the signs and dug-up concrete. Focusing his eyes on the first house, about twenty feet away, he made out a man through the window of the enclosed porch. Although Quinton wasn't able to make out the man's face he could see that he was walking back and forth on the porch with a gun. If he could give his best guess, Quinton would say that it was an AK-47 with a banana clip. Once he saw all that he needed to, he pulled unnoticed away from the block and headed back the way of the hotel. On the drive he couldn't help but think that it had been a good decision to buy the girls new guns.

He pulled up to the hotel an hour later and parked his car in the parking lot that was specifically for guests. The sun had only been up for a short while but the summer heat was already beating down on his forehead. It didn't take him long to grab his overnight bag and start his short walk to the rotating doors. He clicked a button on his keys and waited until he heard his door lock behind him before he vanished inside of the building. Once he got to his room all he wanted to do was enjoy the king-sized bed and the beautiful view, but time wouldn't permit it. Instead he pulled out the travel suit bag from his luggage and tossed it on the bed. Before he got ready to get in the shower he sent both Ahli and Rhonnie a text to make sure they were up: Get ready. We leave in an hour.

"Daddy said hurry up!" Rhonnie read her father's text and summarized it in her own words.

She and Ahli were already back up, thanks to Ahli and her alarm clock. Sometimes Rhonnie felt like her preciseness was a blessing and a curse. A blessing because they were always on time with everything but a curse because Rhonnie would kill to get an extra hour of sleep. She was still sprawled out on the bed while Ahli was in the bathroom of their room taking a shower. Rhonnie had been listening to the constant sound of running water when she felt her phone vibrate beside her head. Deciding that it was time to cut her sister's shower adventures short, she jumped up and grabbed the clothes she would be wearing for the day.

"Ahli!" Rhonnie walked to the bathroom door and tried to turn the knob. She instantly caught an attitude when she found that the door was locked. "If you used up all of the hot water I'm going to be pissed!"

On the other side of the door Ahli heard her sister continuously knocking, but she ignored it. The shower in their hotel room was giving her life and it almost rivaled the one she had in her room at home. She tossed her head back and felt her long, wet hair brush against her shoulder blades. She welcomed the heat and the feeling of the water slapping against her body, and she just stood still for a while.

She glanced down at her curvaceous body and ran a hand down from her stomach to her vaginal opening. The sensuality exuding from the water was reminding her that she hadn't been touched sexually in months. With her other hand she cupped one of her breasts and watched water trickle down her light brown nipple. Closing her eyes she began to imagine that it was Derek. She pretended that her hand was his and she massaged her nipple. Using the middle finger on the hand resting between her legs she began to roll it around her clit. Like a needy woman she accepted the tingles starting to shoot from her head to her toes. Derek wasn't her first lover but he was definitely her best. The two hadn't been in a relationship but they had a bond that was unbreakable, or so Ahli thought.

Derek moved away to go to college and he begged Ahli to come with him. He just couldn't understand why she wanted to stay in a city that had no outlet. There were some aspects in her life that he, of course, never knew about and they were things that she would probably never have told him. But leaving her sister behind was something that she couldn't bear to do; she wouldn't be able to live with herself. She hadn't heard from him since the day he left almost a year ago, and it was crazy to her that thinking about him still broke her heart. He touched her mentally and physically in ways that she didn't even know existed. When they made love there were fireworks every time. She imagined the way he would bury his handsome caramel face in her neck when he stroked deeply. She remembered how his soft hair felt under her fingers while she tried to hold on to him for dear life and not run. His manhood had a slight curve so it hit her G-spot with every thrust.

"Mmm!" Ahli moaned into the steam with her face twisted in pleasure. The thoughts of how his lips felt trailing down her stomach until they reached her tenderness and wrapped around her . . .

"Ahh!" she cried softly, tossing her head back again.

She was experiencing the most extreme orgasm of her life and it felt amazing. Once her body was done quivering she hugged herself and let the water run from her face and into her hair.

"Ahli!"

Her moment was interrupted by Rhonnie banging on the door.

"Hold on!" Ahli yelled back, trying to keep her tone even. "I'm getting out now!"

She washed her body up once more and stepped out onto the white towel she laid down before she got in the tub. It was something her mom always did for them as kids so they wouldn't slip, fall, and "bust their heads to the white meat." She grabbed her towel and put it around her body before she swung the door open.

Rhonnie almost brought her knuckles down on Ahli's nose since she was in the middle of banging on the door again. She stopped at the last minute and Ahli looked at her like she was crazy.

"Here, crybaby." Ahli rolled her eyes at her little sister. She stepped out of the bathroom and a sea of steam followed her. "It's all yours."

Rhonnie set her clothes in the bathroom on the sink and proceeded to shut the door.

"No, leave that open," Ahli said from where she stood in her bra and panties. She reached in her toiletry bag and pulled a comb and brush from it. "I still gotta do my hair."

"You were just in here with the door locked." Rhonnie pretended to smack her lips. "And why you have the door locked anyways? What were you in here doing, playing with your pussy?"

Ahli's face turned red and her expression gave her up instantly. Rhonnie's face twisted up disgustedly and Ahli burst out laughing.

"Mind your damn business!" she said, walking into the bathroom and staring into the mirror. "Hurry up before Daddy fuck us up for fucking up this drop!"

"Uh-huh," Rhonnie said, stripping out of her travel clothes. "Now all of a sudden you're worried about hurrying up. You little nasty!"

It took them about thirty more minutes to get ready. Not knowing what to expect, both girls dressed comfortably, but fly as always. Ahli wore her hair at the top of her head in a ninja bun with her edges laid professionally down. Rhonnie, on the other hand, braided her hair into two long and neat Cherokee braids. That was the only thing different about the two that day, however. Both wore plain black crew-neck T-shirts and baggy tan cargo shorts that stopped right under their knees: the perfect outfit to hide the new toys that their father had given them.

"Pack all of your stuff back up, NaNa," Ahli told her while she threw her dirty clothes back into her bag. "Daddy probably is going to let us take a nap before we go but I want all this shit together so we don't have to worry about it later."

Rhonnie didn't make a retort because she was used to Ahli taking on the role that a mother would. Also, she had come to find over the years that Ahli was right most of the time about most things. Although Rhonnie might bicker and whine, the one thing Ahli would never have to question about her little sister was the level of respect she had for her. Rhonnie would lay her life down for Ahli with no question and Ahli would do the same.

Ahli checked her phone before putting it in her pocket looking to see if she had a missed call from her dad. When she didn't see one she smirked at Rhonnie.

"For once we beat him getting ready," she gloated and went for the door. When she swung it open the smile on her face instantly wiped away.

"Not quite." Quinton grinned down at his daughter from where he stood, leaning on the doorframe. "But almost."

Rhonnie walked passed Ahli, giving her a knowing look, before she stood on her tiptoes to give her dad a peck on the cheek. Ahli rolled her eyes sheepishly and did the same thing. When she stepped back she smoothed the jacket of his black Dolce & Gabbana suit and looked into the eyes she could barely see due to the Cartier sunglasses blessing his face. "Two cars?"

"Nah," Quinton said, thinking about what he saw earlier. The original plan had been to take two vehicles, get in, and get out. But something was telling him that would not be a good idea. "We just need one car for this drop. Get in and get out."

Ahli raised her eyebrow, feeling like her dad was leaving something out, but she didn't press it. Instead she just nodded and let the door go so that it could close behind her. The three of them walked out of the hotel together, with Rhonnie leading, to the gold Camaro. When they were almost there Quinton held his hand out and Ahli tossed the keys to him.

"When we get there under no circumstances are you to reveal that you are my daughters," Quinton told them when he pulled away from the parking lot. He glanced into the rearview mirror as he drove so that he could see Rhonnie. "These men we are meeting with are dangerous and the moment they spot any sign of weakness they will eat you alive. You will be presented to them as my bodyguards."

Rhonnie and Ahli smirked at each other before Rhonnie cocked her head at their father. "Do you think we're green or something?"

"Right," Ahli said from the front seat. "Don't worry about us, Daddy. We know the drill. 'Never reveal who you truly are.' And if anything happens—"

"We pop off," Rhonnie finished for her as she placed her sunglasses over her eyes and faced the window.

Quinton had always been overprotective of his daughters. But ever since he opened the doors of his lifestyle to them he worked hard to keep their connection to him a secret. Not because he was ashamed of being their father but because of the promise he made to Rhebecca when she died. On her deathbed she told him things that he never knew about her and the reasons why she never wanted his name on the birth certificate, nor the correct spelling of her first and last name. She made him promise to keep their girls safe by any means necessary. For years he battled with himself, especially when he lost all access to the money Rhebecca had put up. They struggled because, with the law's eyes already on him, he couldn't work the only job that he knew how to do. However, the things she told him were some of the same things that solidified his decision to teach them all that he knew.

Recently Ahli had begun to ask questions. The death of their mother affected both girls tremendously but it had hit Ahli a little bit harder. She was the firstborn and had a close relationship with her mom. Lately, when alone in her room, she would pull out all of Rhebecca's old stuff just to feel close to her. When she got to all of her own school records an eyebrow was raised for her. Rhebecca's name wasn't on any of it; it was all in Quinton's name. Long before their mother had truly died it was listed that she was not living. She didn't understand that and when she asked her father he brushed it off and said something about getting the girls free lunch. She didn't buy that, not for a second, so she pressed the topic. Eventually he just sighed and told her that one day, when both of the girls were ready, he would tell them. Hearing that, she now knew for a fact that there was a deeper meaning as to why Quinton didn't want anyone to know they were his daughters.

"Exactly." Ahli looked at her father's side profile. "We pop off. As in drop bodies, snatch souls. Daddy, hopefully after all of this you see that we are big girls and can handle some words. I think we are ready to hear whatever it is you're hiding."

Quinton didn't flinch; he kept driving almost like he didn't hear a word Ahli said. But Rhonnie did.

"Daddy, what is she talking about?" She leaned over since she was sitting behind him. Looking at the side of his face she searched for an answer there. "You hiding stuff from us?"

There weren't many times that Quinton was stern or even raised his voice at his daughters, but right then he took the same tone he would with someone who'd crossed him. "You are my children, not the other way around. When I am ready to tell you, I will tell you. Until then I'm not at liberty to tell you anything. Remember whose blood runs through your veins."

His voice was cold and it instantly stopped any question from even being thought of. Ahli knew not to press the matter and Rhonnie leaned back into her seat. The car was quiet and no one spoke until they reached a battered neighborhood. Their father made a couple of twists and turns until finally they reached their destination.

"It looks like we're going to have to find another way in." Rhonnie leaned forward when she saw the construction all down the street they needed to turn down.

"No, we don't," Quinton said, and turned down the street despite all of the construction signs. He only drove as far as the first house and the moment he put the car in park there was a kid walking to the car with a suspicious look on his face. The young man looked to be Ahli's age and was dressed in a pair of Levi's with a white V-neck Ralph Lauren T-shirt with a blue Polo logo. His hair was faded into a flat top that was a couple of inches tall with blond tips. His face would be handsome had it not been for the fact that he wore a mug that let Rhonnie know that not many people were welcome on that block.

"You lost?" the kid asked when he got to the Camaro. He knelt down and peered into the car so that he could give them all eye contact. His eyes lingered on Ahli and she mugged him back letting him know she wasn't intimidated. Rhonnie leaned into her window so she could check him out a little better. The bulges in the back of his pants showed that he was strapped, most likely with something automatic.

"Not at all," Quinton told the kid, giving his hard face a small smile. "Dot is expecting me. Tell him I'm here to bring his bitches home."

The kid looked curiously in Quinton's face before nodding slightly and backing away from the window.

"Yeah, a'ight," he said, pulling a walkie-talkie from one of his pockets.

While he was doing that Ahli looked directly in front of her at the rest of the neighborhood, if you could call it that. There were cars in a few of the driveways of the old houses but not many. She wasn't stupid though, she would bet money that each of the vehicles had bodies with loaded weapons in them watching to see who the newcomers were.

A slight movement caught her eye. She squinted her eyes and focused on the yellow house three houses down. "Rhonnie," she said in a low tone and nodded toward the house. "Look."

Rhonnie, too, squinted to the house and sure enough she saw the sniper knelt behind a plant on the porch. She chuckled to herself and shook her head. "It's like Little Italy in here."

"A'ight, y'all good," the kid said, coming back to the car and pointing his finger down the street. "Pull up to that brick house in the middle."

"A'ight," Quinton said, putting the car back in drive.

"What's your name?" Ahli asked before Quinton pulled off.

"Brayland," he said, staring into her eyes.

"Well, Brayland, tell your people that if they want a more effective defense then it's better to not give away their location," she said, glancing toward the sniper again. "I can guarantee there is one in the exact same place in the house across the street. Also the cars are just out of place. I can bet that you have shooters in every vehicle. If we were on that"—she winked—"your whole operation would have been penetrated that easy. Oh, and I like your hair."

Brayland was taken aback and, before he even had a rebuttal lined up, the Camaro pulled away from him. Quinton smirked to himself and couldn't help but be proud of his daughter's keen eyes. He didn't know why he had ever doubted them in the first place.

He did as Brayland said and pulled to the brick house in the middle of the neighborhood. The house was two stories and definitely the best looking house on the block. The yard was neatly trimmed and there were shooters lined up neatly around the whole perimeter of the house with their guns drawn. Before the car could be swarmed he and the girls stepped out of it, understanding that there would be no valet. A heavyset man carrying an Uzi as casually as a cell phone walked up on Quinton with three men close behind him. He was slightly shorter so he had to cock his head up.

"You here to see Dot about some bitches?"

"That's what I said, ain't it?" Quinton said in a bored tone.

"Well?" The man shrugged his shoulders and sarcastically looked around. "Where they at then?"

"You Dot?" When the man didn't say anything Quinton looked past him. "What are we still talking for then?"

The ugly man with the dreads stood firm in front of him and didn't budge, even though a part of him felt that it was a mistake. The vibe Quinton gave off was that of a man not to be tampered with, and even though he couldn't see the eyes behind the glasses he felt the cold gaze. The men behind the dread-head all tensed up, and tightened their grips around their weapons.

"Let him through," a voice called, interrupting the tension between the opposing sides. "This isn't how you treat our guests!"

"Because we don't have guests, Dot," the dread-head said, still staring up into Quinton's emotionless face. "You taught me that." He moved out of the way to let the three newcomers through before he gave the others the signal to go back to their posts.

"You must be Dot," Quinton said, bounding up the few steps on the stoop.

The man standing in the doorway of the house had a forty ounce of beer in one hand and a stack of hundreds in the other. He was a good-looking man who seemed to be in his mid-thirties with long hair that was pulled back into a braided ponytail. His skin was bronze and he had a mustache that connected to his neatly trimmed beard. His sharp brown eyes pierced the three people walking toward him. When he saw that instead of an array of men there were only two women with his connection he was shocked. Not only were they women, they were young women. One couldn't have been older than twenty-one and the other looked to be about eighteen.

"And you must be Quinton," Dot said, raising a hand so Quinton could shake it. "And who are these two beautiful ladies might I ask?"

"My bodyguards." Quinton smirked and pulled his hand back. "Don't let their age or beautiful exterior fool you. They're thorough as they come."

Dot could already see their loyalty to Quinton in their stance. The cargos they wore were a dead giveaway that they were armed and the calmness in their presence let him know that they were dangerous. Still, two women barely posed a threat to his army.

"Come, let us do business. Get this shit over with." Dot waved them in the house.

Rhonnie and Ahli had seen a lot of things in their lives but a trap house was not one of them. Ever since they'd purchased their house they barely visited the hood. Most of their licks were done in nice neighborhoods, the ones where, even if unplanned, they knew they would be leaving with something worth a couple bands. There, at that moment, they found out that the things they saw on TV were true. As they walked through the house they passed the entrance to the living room and saw that there were half-naked women bagging up drugs on the living room floor. Dot led them to the kitchen where two women in nothing but their red lace bra and panties were sitting at an island. Not once did they look up from the money they were counting. The men who had followed them inside stopped in the hallway outside of the kitchen and lined up with their backs to the walls.

"If you have what I need your money is right here. One hundred thousand dollars. May I?" Dot said, taking a swig of his beer before setting it on a countertop. He then motioned to the bags that the young women had on their shoulders.

Rhonnie looked to Ahli, who nodded. Rhonnie unzipped the duffle bag that she was holding just enough to reach in and grab one of the bricks.

"Catch," she said and threw it to Dot.

Dot took a sharp knife from one of the drawers and made a small puncture in the kilo. He took a small amount from it and steadied it on the tip of the blade.

"Yup," he said, nodding after he snorted the cocaine. "This that good shit right here. I want all of them."

"I thought you would say that." Quinton nodded, satisfied.

"At first I was skeptical," Dot admitted, setting the kilo on the island behind him. "But I should have known that Lance wouldn't let me down."

"Never," Quinton agreed. "Lance is a man of his word. Always has been."

Dot gave Quinton a look that wasn't easily readable before he turned his head to the women sitting on the stools.

"Bag up this man's money," he instructed. "I'm sure he has better things to do besides stare at you two hoes all day."

Ahli stood back and watched all of her surroundings like a hawk. There was not much talk between Quinton and Dot, and the deal went very smoothly. Once the swap had been made Dot and Quinton shook hands one more time.

"If you stay you should come through this little party my people are throwing downtown tonight," Dot offered. "Your bodyguards are welcome to come, too."

He winked at Ahli and she instantly turned her nose up at him.

"A generous offer, but honestly we have no further business in your city after this," Quinton graciously declined, holding up the suitcase of money in his hand.

"Understood." Dot smiled. He picked his beer back up and took another swig. "You know, any other man wouldn't be able to walk out of here alive if they wouldn't have taken their sunglasses off. If they wouldn't have looked me in the eyes like a man."

Ahli felt Rhonnie tense up behind her. She too heard the bitterness in Dot's voice and didn't know what to make of it. Instinctively she put her hand around the butt of the gun behind her back. All she needed was for Quinton to say the word and she'd let all her rounds go. But Quinton didn't flinch.

"Any other man wouldn't have even granted me entrance with these sunglasses still on my face." Quinton's voice was smooth. "So what is it that you are trying to say?"

The vein on Dot's temple pulsed slightly and Ahli thought for sure that Quinton struck a nerve. For a second he said nothing; his eyes just went from Quinton, then to Ahli, and they stopped on Rhonnie.

"Nothing," he finally responded. "Nothing at all."

Not waiting another second for him to say anything else out of pocket to her father, Rhonnie took the first steps to leave the way they had come. Ahli gave Dot one last look before she followed her dad and the suitcase of money. The tension in the air was so thick that you could cut it with a knife and Ahli's only focus was making sure her family got out of that house with no issue. She didn't even relax when they were all in the car and the money was in the back seat resting peacefully next to Rhonnie. She didn't inhale an unbothered breath of air until they were a few blocks away from the neighborhood.

"Daddy, something don't feel right," Ahli said, shaking her head. "You see how he was staring at us?"

"I know." Quinton was already making arrangements for an early checkout.

To him the aura throughout the whole deal had been off. There was something in Dot's eyes that didn't sit right with him and it was enough to make him want to head home as soon as possible. He trusted Lance, but even he had said Dot was a man of many traits. Quinton just hoped that being a snake businessman wasn't one of them.

"I don't even give a fuck about sleeping," Rhonnie said. She too was feeling uneasy. "Something was off about all of them niggas; they weren't right. How does Uncle Lance know these people?"

"He didn't say," Quinton said, speeding toward the hotel. "And right now I don't care. All I know is that we're about to get the hell out of Miami."

Chapter 4

"That nigga brought bitches here as protection?" the dread-head man, who went by the name Tank, said. He and four other men sat on the porch of the brick house watching the gold Camaro when it drove off. He took a long drag of the blunt in his hand and shook his head when the car was out of sight. He couldn't believe that Dot had just let them drive off. That lick would have been too easy.

"I don't know, man," Brayland said. "There was something about those three."

"Yeah, they both had big old booties!" Tank said and dapped the other men up. "Dot shoulda just kept the money and took the work. Bodied all three of them muhfuckas. They were asking to get peeled off. Who the fuck comes to a nigga like Dot only three deep?"

"People who only need to be three deep," Brayland said matter-of-factly. "Strength ain't always in numbers, my nigga."

He thought back to the words the older of the two girls had said to him. She wasn't in the block for more than two minutes and already mentally penetrated their whole defensive system. If they would have come in with more than three people and they were as calculated as her, he knew they would be fighting a losing battle if something popped off.

"Fuck that," Tank said, hitting the blunt in his hand. "We should have robbed them and kept the money. That would have been more money in our pockets."

"Come on, man." Brayland chuckled at the thirst in his friend. "Ain't no honor in that."

"I'm a dope boy. Ain't no honor in a lot of the shit I do."

Brayland could tell that there was no getting through to Tank. Instead he took the blunt and hit it a couple of times, tuning out the men and their plots. He understood where Tank was coming from. Tank was a man who came from a long line of crackheads and hustlers. In his family you had no choice but to choose one of the sides, so the game was all he knew. For Tank, his loyalty would lie with whoever had the most money and manpower. He just wanted to be on the winning side.

Brayland, on the other hand, was different. He was introduced to the game the same way Tank had been; the only difference was the streets didn't raise Brayland. He, unlike so many other young black men in his neighborhood, had a father who taught him everything he needed to know about the hustle. When Brayland's mother ran off with a white man his dad never once slacked on his parenting.

Brayland's father, Larry Michaels, was a college graduate with a degree in finance. He was the one a person called when they didn't know how to balance their outlandish spending habits with real-life needs. Money was his forte. When he found the first ounce of weed in Brayland's bedroom along with the scale and Baggies he wasn't mad. Nor was he mad when he found the eight-balls of coke in his dresser next to the wad of cash. He did something Brayland didn't expect. He sat him down and told Brayland how proud of him he was. "If it's in your heart, do it."

Larry told Brayland that if he was going to hustle illegally then he had better be smart about it. The first lesson was to never shit where you eat. He told Brayland that by no means should his work be near the place he laid his head. The second lesson was money cleansing. In Brayland's profession the money he received was tax free and dirty. The only way he'd be able to spend it comfortably would be to clean it with a legitimate business. Which was why Brayland himself graduated college with a degree in business management. The third lesson embedded in Brayland's mind was loyalty. Only go against those who cross you. If they don't do anything to hurt you never go out waging war. Never make unnecessary enemies, and keep good people around you. If their heart didn't match his then there was no reason being in cahoots. Despite the job, Larry told his son nothing that he had would be blessed if he never put out goodness into the world.

They were things that Brayland had lost sight of over the past few years. When Larry died from a blood clot in his heart Brayland submerged himself in his work. He was always on the block making moves because he didn't know how to handle losing the one parent he had left. He had even stopped the process of starting up his own business because he didn't have anyone to make proud any longer. He was just another street mutt in the eyes of the law and he didn't care. As long as he was a street mutt with a pocket full of hundreds.

It wasn't until he looked into the eyes of the beautiful woman with the bun on her head that he was reminded of who he used to be. He sat on the porch with the other fellas as long as he could, listening to them talk about the sick things they would have done to the two women if Dot made them stay. The way they were talking it made a person believe that they didn't get any pussy on a regular.

"Man, y'all wild," Brayland said, hitting the blunt one last time. "Watch the block. I gotta piss."

He felt his high creeping up on him and taking him to the place in the clouds where he belonged. Inside of the house he went toward the bathroom on the first level. His bladder was so full that if he didn't relieve it of all the liquid inside it was sure to explode.

"Man, what the fuck?" he said to himself when he tried the bathroom doorknob and saw that the door was locked.

"Yup, and I'm takin' a shit, too!" a voice called from the bathroom. "Take ya ass on upstairs."

Brayland didn't stand by the door long enough to hear that last part; he was already halfway to the staircase. Passing the entrance to the living room he heard a couple of the bitches who were bagging up the coke call his name. Brayland didn't know it, but they all wanted a piece of him. The other men Dot had working for him jumped at every opportunity to run up in their juicy goodness, but when it came to Brayland all he saw was a bunch of coked-out females. He respected his manhood so there was no way he would stick his dick inside of a female who didn't take care of her womanhood.

He ignored their voices and bounded up the stairs, two at a time. The bathroom upstairs was smack dab in the middle of two bedrooms and he swore he heard the fat lady sing when he saw the door open and the light off. He didn't look into either of the two rooms; he was just worried about handling his business. He flipped on the light and shut the door to let anyone else who potentially had to use it know it was occupied. As soon as the door was locked behind him he unzipped his pants, pulled his nine inches of thickness through the hole in his Ralph Lauren boxers, and emptied his bladder.

"Ahhh." He threw his head back in relief with his eyes closed.

When his bladder was completely empty he shook the tip and zipped his pants back up. After he flushed the toilet he washed his hands vigorously in the white jail-like sink. Turning the faucet off he made to leave the bathroom, but he heard something that caught his attention and made him stop mid-step.

"Lance is my man but this shit is just too easy."

Being that it was an older house every wall in it was thin. Brayland could make out every word that Dot was saying in the room to the right of him.

"How you think they got their hands on coke that good?" A voice that Brayland knew as Drew said.

"It was acquired," Dot said.

"Stolen?"

"Most likely. There is only one cartel that carries product this rich. The Last Kings."

"They stole from the Last Kings?"

Brayland heard the fear in Drew's voice and he himself stopped breathing. The Last Kings to a grown man was equivalent to the boogeyman to a child. They were as ruthless as they came and the last thing he knew Dot wanted was to harbor their stolen product.

"I don't know," Dot said. "And honestly I don't care. I paid for these bricks so in my eyes they are mine."

"I feel like you have somethin' else to say, cuz."

"If these bitches are this good, I want more."

Their voices got slightly quieter making Brayland go to the wall and put his ear to it so that he could hear the rest of what they were saying.

"Well, you gon' have to wait until we flip these bitches then. 'Cause you just spent all the re-up money on these muhfuckas right here. I can have the corner boys work some overtime to get it off."

"Nah. I'm not a patient man. This is something you should know. If these bricks we have are stolen I don't want it to even be known that I have them. And if I don't want them traced back to me that means I have to eliminate the sale and get my money back."

"And use that to double up on the product." Brayland heard the smile in Drew's voice. "I like how you think, cuz."

"Word up. I'm always two steps ahead of all these niggas in the game. It's the only way to keep the cycle going. When they were in the house I had a tracker put on their car. This man came into a lion's den with sheep; he was asking for this to happen. Load up; we're about to head out now."

"What about Lance?"

"Throw that nigga a couple extra stacks for setting up this lick."

Brayland exited the bathroom in a hurry not wanting them to know he'd heard everything they said. Drew was Dot's cousin and, besides Brayland, he was his best shooter. Drew and Dot were as thick as thieves so Brayland knew that if Dot said the word go there was no question after that. He went back down to the porch and sat back in the chair he had just gotten up from.

"Damn, nigga," Tank said when he saw him. "Did your high ass fall in or somethin'? I finished that blunt and twisted up another one since you been gone."

When Brayland didn't say anything back Tank shrugged it off and lit his blunt. Brayland's thoughts were coming to him a hundred miles an hour and he barely heard what Tank said to him. Any other time he wouldn't care about the way that Dot did business but right then he was bothered. This was the man he worked for. The same time Brayland was filling his own pockets he was putting more money in Dot's. This was the man they helped keep on top of the game and if Larry could see his son now he would be disappointed.

"Never make unnecessary enemies."

His father's voice crept to his mind and echoed there. These people just brought Dot a means to save his ever-fluctuating business and in return he was going to rob and kill them. That wasn't a businessman, or a man for that matter. That sounded like a con artist and a snake. Like somebody who would turn on anyone, no matter how much work had been put in for him.

The front door opened and out walked Dot and his cousin Drew. "I need you little niggas to hold down the fort until I get back," Dot said.

Drew reached to dap everybody up but when he got to Brayland his hand was extended longer than he would have liked before he got a dap back. A funny look came across Drew's light-skinned face and he brushed the waves on his head. "You good, young'un?"

"I'm straight."

"You sure? 'Cause a part of me felt like you ain't want to dap ya big bro up."

"I didn't," Brayland told him bluntly. "And since when were you my big brother?"

Brayland didn't give either one of the men eye contact; instead he just glared at the neighborhood in front of him. Drew wanted to floor the kid and his arm flexed slightly.

"Come on, nigga," Dot said, checking the clips on the guns at his waist. A big black Suburban full of Dot's men pulled up in front of the house. "It's time to head out."

"We gon' talk when I get back," Drew threatened, pointing a finger at Brayland's face.

"Yeah, a'ight, man," Brayland said, leaning back in his chair.

If looks could kill Brayland would have dropped dead from the plastic white chair he was sitting in. Out of all of Dot's shooters Brayland had always been the most arrogant. Drew told Dot that he needed to handle that kid before he got out of hand but Dot never listened. He would say that his nonchalant attitude was what made him a great asset to the team. Drew turned his back on the porch and went to take his seat in Dot's BMW when he pulled it behind the Suburban.

"Them niggas gonna go put in work on somebody," Tank acknowledged. "Man, why they ain't pull me to go?"

"On God!"

Tank was slapping hands with another man when Brayland stood and bounded down the porch steps. Brayland realized at that moment that he was surrounded by a bunch of jokers. Nothing Dot had would be blessed and it was something that he'd been noticing for a while now. There was no reason to stay down for a man who was only down for himself.

"Where you going, nigga?" Tank called after him. "Dot told us to watch the block."

"So watch the block then," Brayland told him and kept walking.

Chapter 5

"No questions. Grab everything you came with and meet me back out here in five minutes."

Quinton wasted no time in barking out orders when he pulled back into the parking lot of the hotel. He parked the car a few spaces away from his own and the girls wasted no time in hopping out. They heard the seriousness in Quinton's voice and knew that it would be best if they did as they were told.

When they took off toward the building Quinton smoothly relocated the briefcases of money to the trunk of his car. His bags had already been placed there long before they'd left to make the deal in the first place. He stood by the girls' car and waited for them to come back out. Instinct told him to check his surroundings. The scenery seemed normal: families checking into the hotel, bellhops carrying bags. Still, something was off in the air and he couldn't shake the bad feeling he had in his stomach. Something wasn't right and Quinton mentally rewound to when they walked out of Dot's house. At the time he didn't think anything of the men walking from the car but the more he envisioned it the more off the whole scene seemed. There was no reason for anyone to be as close to their vehicle as they were, especially if Dot was just going to let them go. *Unless* . . .

A thought entered his mind and his chest tightened. "Shit," Quinton said when took a few steps back toward the girls' car.

He bent down and saw that his inkling had been correct. He reached his hand under the Camaro and pulled a small black device from one of the axels. There was a small red light blinking in the top right corner of it and he took a brisk breath.

"Shit!" he said again, throwing the tracking device.

He should have known not to leave the vehicle unattended. Thinking fast he walked back to where his trunk was still wide open and he pushed the briefcases and bags back. Most people kept their spare tires in the trunk; not Quinton. He lifted the trick floor and revealed the secret gun storage he had there. On his hip he already had a Glock 9 and from the trunk he pulled out a black AR-15. He calculated that they maybe had a few minutes before they were found, but when the first black truck turned into the parking lot he realized that he miscalculated. Slamming his trunk closed, he knelt down and prepared for war.

"Hurry up, NaNa," Ahli said, jogging behind her little sister.

Booking rooms on the first floor proved to be a smart move. They bustled past the people in the lobby trying to check in and, once no eyes were on them, they ran as fast as they could back through the revolving doors.

"I'm glad I listened to you about packing my stuff," Rhonnie said as she ran with her bag on her shoulder. "It made this so much fas—"

Ahli pressed her hand to Rhonnie's chest, interrupting her statement. At first Rhonnie was confused, but when she directed her eyesight to what had made Ahli stop in the first place, she understood.

"Who is that?" Rhonnie asked, squinting her eyes at the all-black vehicles that had just skirted into the parking lot.

The cars unloaded quickly, and there were at least a dozen men all holding guns. When the door to the BMW opened she instantly recognized the person who got out the driver's side as Dot. Rhonnie knew then that her father had been right. Dot scanned the whole lot and, once he spotted the car he was looking for, he gave the order with a simple hand gesture.

"Daddy!" Ahli screamed when the men pointed their guns and started dumping bullets into the Camaro. "No!"

It looked and sounded like the Fourth of July outside of that hotel. People were clinging to each other and running everywhere but toward the gunshots. The screams in the air were drowned out by the weapons and Ahli knew there was no surviving all of those bullets. The car looked like a piece of cheese once they were done with it. Her heart sank to her stomach because she was certain her father had been in the car still. She let the bag on her shoulder go and stood her ground as the men, women, and children ran wild around her. Both she and Rhonnie pulled the guns from their waists, preparing to take off toward Dot's gunmen. The moment they went to take their first steps a strong set of hands gripped their shoulders and yanked them back.

"Are you stupid?"

Relief swarmed over both girls. They would recognize Quinton's voice anywhere.

"Daddy!" Rhonnie exclaimed. "I thought—"

"No time for that, NaNa," Quinton said and pointed to his car. "They don't know that's my car. We have to steer them away from it so that we can get to it. Got it?"

"Yes." Ahli already understood what he was saying and knew it was her turn. "Rhonnie, I need you be the decoy. I won't be able to get over there unless they're all distracted. Daddy, you cover her and give me the keys. We have to move quick because once they see that they didn't hit shit they're going to try to light this entire place up."

She didn't wait for either of them to respond because, like Quinton said, there was no time. She ducked behind cars as she ran and tried to get as close to her father's car as possible.

"Come on, NaNa," she urged as she watched the men run up on the still-smoking Camaro.

She peeked, while ducked down, through the window of an old Pontiac Grand Prix at the scene five cars away.

"Boss!" she heard one of Dot's shooters shout out. "It's empty. Ain't nobody in there!"

"Look around!" Dot barked. "They're here somewhere and I want my money!"

Snake! Ahli thought when she realized Dot was trying to hit them all with the okie-doke.

"I thought you were a businessman!"

Ahli stopped breathing when she heard her sister's voice. All eyes suddenly turned to where Rhonnie stood in an open row before them. "You should be ashamed of yourself. This isn't how real men conduct business!"

Before they could even get a grip on what was happening, Rhonnie had already opened fire on all of them. Her first bullet connected sickly with the head of a man standing in front of Dot and his neck snapped back viciously. His blood sprayed the men around him, but that didn't stop them from firing back. Rhonnie clipped two more of Dot's shooters before she suddenly stopped shooting and took off the other way.

"Come on," Rhonnie said to herself as she willed her legs to go faster down the aisle.

Each car she came up on was intact at first but once she passed them they were infiltrated with bullet holes. Dot's shooters were sending undisciplined shots her way and not connecting with their intended target. Rhonnie just hoped her luck wouldn't run out before she made it to the green Ford Explorer that Quinton was knelt behind.

"Now, Daddy!"

Dot's men didn't even see it coming; they ran straight into a trap. Once he saw Rhonnie jump out of the way, Quinton used the element of surprise as his weapon. He saw that there were five men shooting after Rhonnie while four had stayed behind to cloak Dot.

"She over there! Get that bitch!"

The men never got the chance to send another bullet in her direction. Quinton shot five calculated bullets at the men's knees and they all hit their marks. When they fell from the pain Rhonnie didn't give them the chance to figure out what had just happened. She emptied her clip one bullet at a time into their heads.

"Leak," she said and spat at their bleeding, dead bodies before she turned to her father. She waved her gun at him. "Daddy, I'm out!"

"Here!" he said, tossing her the pistol he wasn't using. "Watch your back. We need to get to the car!"

Rhonnie opened her mouth to respond but she was cut off guard by the sound of rapid fire. Her body snapped back and she felt a pain that she had never experienced before in life. Her face twisted into a grimace as she fell to the ground. Her blood blended in with that of the dead men lying beside her and her hand clutched her wound.

"Uhhh!" She gasped with her eyes clenched shut.

"Rhonnie!" Quinton's eyes widened when he saw his daughter drop to the ground.

He knelt down and looked up in time to see two men advancing on them with their weapons drawn. Quinton refused to let them get any closer to Rhonnie than they already had. His gun barked and he put his body between the men and Rhonnie, not caring if they opened his body up with their bullets. His trigger finger twitched repeatedly and he didn't care where his bullets found homes. He didn't know which one of them was the cause of Rhonnie being sprawled out, but one of them hit his baby so both of them had to pay. He heard sirens in the distance but paid them no mind. He was so focused on the men in front of him that he didn't notice the man who had gone around, only to pop up behind him and Rhonnie.

Rhonnie was too hurt to move; it felt like the bullet in her shoulder had shattered. She saw the menacing smile creep up on the light-skinned kid's face as he aimed his gun into her face. She knew she was a goner and she mentally sent her love to Ahli and her dad. Her eyelids began to lower and she welcomed death. Before her eyes were all the way shut she heard a final shot ring out and surprisingly she felt no more pain. Instead, she saw a swift bullet enter the kid's right temple and come out through the left. The shocked look on his ugly face was priceless when he slumped to the concrete.

"She got the car. Go! Go!"

Rhonnie felt a strong set of arms scoop her up from the ground and, although she tried to focus on the person's face, everything around her was a blur. She had lost too much blood and mentally was threatening to tap out.

"Stay with me, ma," the masculine voice was saying to her while he ran with her. "Come on. Stay with me."

Rhonnie couldn't get a grip on the scenery around her, but she heard the sound of tires coming to a stop on gravel not too far ahead.

"Get in . . . No. Oh my God. NaNa! No!" Rhonnie heard Ahli's crushed voice. "My sister. Rhonnie!"

"She straight!" the man's voice said. "We gotta go!"

"We?"

"Yes, we!" Rhonnie heard Quinton's voice butt in. "This young nigga just saved our lives. Get in, kid!"

Rhonnie felt the stickiness of the hot leather seat under her body, but that didn't put a stop to her pain or the fact that she was bleeding out.

"Fuck, Daddy!" she groaned when the she heard the door shut. Her eyes were on the light at the top of the car until it turned off. "Why didn't you tell me getting shot hurt so bad?"

"Because I've never been shot before," Quinton said, reaching back to grip Rhonnie's hand. "Hang in there. We ain't out of the hot water yet."

"Hell nah," the other man said. "Dot got a whole 'nother sweep coming through this bitch. And they don't give a fuck about no cop so don't think those flashing lights are the cavalry."

"Brayland, is it?"

"Yeah." Brayland nodded and tried to adjust Rhonnie's head to a comfortable position in his lap.

"Did Dot see you?"

"Yeah," Brayland said. "I shot his right-hand man in the chest so she could get to the car. He fell into Dot when he went down."

"You can't go back then."

"Nope."

"Then show us how to get the fuck out of here!"

Ahli maneuvered the vehicle in such a way it would have been thought that she drove for NASCAR. The parking lot had three exits: two where they just were, and one in the front of the building. The two closest to them were blocked, one by Dot's shooters and one by the police. It seemed that everyone was gunning for the black Mercedes, so Ahli had only once choice.

"Hold on!" Ahli shouted and hit a U-turn while going sixty miles per hour.

The only way to the front of the building was through the lobby. She ducked her head down when she hit the revolving door, causing the glass in the whole front of the building to shatter. Quinton's windows were barely scratched due to the custom Gorilla Glass all around the vehicle.

Thump! Thump! Thump! Thump! Thump! Thump!

Ahli pressed her foot down on the gas when the automatic rounds attacked the vehicle from behind. She refused to look in the rearview mirror because the last thing she needed when her sister lay bleeding out in the back seat was to get intimidated by the enemy.

"Get the fuck out of the way!" she screamed and honked her horn at the hotel's guests. She knew they were terrified but she refused to slow the car down, so whoever got hit would just get hit. "Daddy!"

"Already on it, baby girl!" Quinton set the AR-15 down and opened the glove compartment so that he could switch to his Uzi. Rolling his window down he pointed the gun out of it.

"Aim for the tires," Brayland told him, straining his neck to look behind him.

Quinton took his advice and took out the left tire on the Suburban tailing them throughout the lobby. The driver lost control of the vehicle and swerved wildly until it finally crashed into a concrete water fountain.

"Hold on!" Ahli yelled when she drove through the back end of the hotel.

The sound of the doors coming off the hinges and shattering glass was deafening. The car bounced and rocked crazily as she drove on top of the grass until she hopped the curb, finding her place in the traffic. A couple of cars swerved to avoid an impact but that was the least of Ahli's worries. They all looked behind the Mercedes at the damage they caused at the hotel.

"Damn," Brayland said, shaking his head. "Y'all fucked that place up. I hope y'all didn't use your real names."

"Daddy," Rhonnie groaned again. "I'm going to die."

"Shut the fuck up saying stupid shit, little girl!" Ahli yelled. "Daddy, is anybody following us?"

"No," Quinton said, glancing back at the smoky scene one last time. "Brayland, put pressure on her shoulder. LaLa, hop on the interstate, get off at the first exit, and pop the trunk."

"W . . . why?"

"We can't take her to the hospital." Quinton stared back at his daughter's perspiring face. He grimaced knowing that, without a real doctor, getting the bullet out would be even more painful than one going in. "But we gotta get that bullet out. I have a first aid kit in the trunk."

Chapter 6

"Come on over here, sugar," a sweet, sexy voice purred into a dimly lit room. "Don't you want to join us in this bed?"

The voice belonged to a pale woman with red freckles and red curly hair. She lay naked on a round king-sized bed, in what was called the "Fun Room," alongside a brown-skinned beauty. The room was big and fully furnished with white dressers, a white bearskin rug, and a mirror that almost completely covered the ceiling. To the far right there was a window seat and in front of it was a stripper pole.

Both women looked on with hungry eyes at the tall, muscular white man standing at the foot of the bed. On one side of the bed there was a table with many kinky toys: whips, strap-ons, chains, and handcuffs. On the other side of the bed there were edibles: whipped cream, strawberries, and warm chocolate syrup.

"What will tonight's poison be, Mr. Clark?" the brown-skinned beauty whispered with low, seductive eyes. "Are you feeling naughty or nice?"

Braxton Clark, a district judge, undid the cufflinks on his white dress shirt and loosened his blue tie. He knew the last place he should have been was in that room with those two women; yet, there he was, preparing to give their pussies the wrecking of a lifetime. Staring down at their perky breasts and round bottoms he thanked the heavens for coming across what looked to be a simple hotel for travelers.

The first time he'd ever driven through the small Iowa town he almost didn't stop. He was on his way home to Nebraska from an important business trip and he wanted nothing more than to lie in his bed next to his wife. But it was almost midnight at the time and his eyes were barely staying open. His bank account had just gotten another six figures added to it and if he drove off the road due to falling asleep at the wheel he'd never be able to enjoy it. To his luck he came up on what seemed to be an okay-looking two-story hotel in the middle of nowhere. A man of his caliber usually would never stay in a place like that, but he knew he might have had to drive another twenty minutes before he would come upon a better hotel. The lights were on so that signified that they were in business; and he would have never guessed that one visit would lead to many more.

"I'm feeling like a little of both." He gave them a slick smile. "But first I'm feeling like experiencing the reversed Oreo. Can you do that for me, baby?" He directed his question to the brown-skinned woman, who returned his gaze sexily and licked her lips.

"Anything for you, Mr. Clark." She turned to the white woman and placed one finger to her cherry lips. Gently, she pushed her head back toward the plush pillow behind her. "Lie on your back, Diamond. Mr. Clark wants me to taste you. Okay?"

"Okay, Anna."

As Diamond lay back Anna let her hand slide down the front of her body, until Diamond was completely on her back and Anna's hand was on top of her navel. Right before Mr. Clark's monthly appointment Anna had taken a few shots of Patrón and the buzz had finally hit her. Being under the influence was the only way that she could be attracted to Diamond. Not because she wasn't pretty; Diamond was a very attractive and well-stacked woman. It was just that having sex with the other women at the illegal brothel was never something Anna planned to do, no matter how good she was at it. But if it pleased Madame then she would do it.

"Touch her breasts," Mr. Clark demanded. "I want to watch your tongue lick her nipples. Slowly."

Anna did as she was told. She positioned herself in between Diamond's legs and fondled both of Diamond's breasts in her hands. Diamond closed her eyes and moaned softly when Anna began to roll her nipples between her delicate and freshly manicured fingers. Anna looked back at Mr. Clark, who had removed his pants and underwear completely. She smirked devilishly at him and slowly arched her back, giving him a front-row view of her newly shaved vagina. If possible, seven inches of thickness grew another couple of centimeters when she wrapped her full lips around Diamond's pink areola. He was frozen in place watching the girl-on-girl scene at hand and he stroked himself a little faster. The sound of Anna's lips slurping on Diamond's breasts was almost too much for him to handle and he took a brisk breath. His wife would probably divorce him if she knew that these two women pleased his dick on a regular basis. If only she knew that they were the ones who were saving their marriage in the first place. It was because of these pleasantly nasty women that he so happily went home. All he needed was one fix and he was good for a whole month.

"Mmmm!" Diamond moaned and squirmed under Anna when she felt a finger tickling her wet clit. She thrust her body up and down and squeezed her vaginal walls. "Anna. Fuck me with your fingers. Please?"

"Please?" Anna asked, snapping her lips from Diamond's right nipple, causing a ripple effect. "You want my fingers in you, baby?"

"Yes," Diamond breathed. "I'm so horny. I need you to fuck me with your fingers."

"You mean like this?"

Anna shoved two fingers inside of Diamond's wetness and pushed them as deep as she could. Instantly, she felt Diamond's walls clench, but that didn't stop her from retracting her fingers only to shove them deep inside again. Anna placed her hand on Diamond's stomach when her back arched and she tried to scoot back.

"Hell nah," Anna taunted, licking one of Diamond's nipples. "This is what you wanted right? Huh?"

She forced Diamond to take every plunge her fingers made into her gushy love spot until she felt the first quiver come about. The alcohol was making her feel extra freaky, nastier than she had ever been before. That extra shot she'd taken had Anna wanting nothing more than to catch every drop of Diamond's juice on her tongue. Quickly she removed her fingers, slid down, and replaced them with her mouth. Her hands found homes on the outside of each one of Diamond's thighs as she buried her head between her thick, pale legs. She licked and sucked on Diamond's pussy until she had no choice but to come all over her face. Anna didn't have time to relish in the fact of how surprisingly turned on she was by Diamond's throbbing clit. From behind her she hadn't heard Mr. Clark come up, but she sure felt it when he rammed himself inside of her drippy opening.

"Keep licking her pussy," Mr. Clark panted, forcing Anna's head back between Diamonds legs. "Make her scream your name while your scream mine!"

He pumped in and out of Anna like his life depended on it and sure enough the room was filled with jumbled cries of pleasure within moments. Mr. Clark, of course, wore a condom but the whole time he fought the urge to take it off and force his shaft in Anna's wet pussy, only to use it as lube so that he could jam it into her thick ass.

"This ass," he moaned into the air, feeling the buildup coming.

There was something about the way it shook whenever he dug into her and pulled back out. Out of both girls he loved fucking Anna the most. His eyes were glued on how her opening swallowed the tip of his penis and spit it back out. He had to dig his nails into her thighs for the orgasm he experienced. He released what seemed like a load of semen into the condom he wore, but he refused to stop fucking the brown goddess until he was completely soft. Throwing his head back in pure bliss he smacked one of her cheeks; and then he squeezed one of Diamond's thighs.

"You two are going to be the death of me," he breathed and plopped down on the bed.

"Mmm," Diamond said, winking at Anna. "Only if your wife is going to share the insurance money."

Mr. Clark chuckled and pointed to one of the white dressers. "Speaking of money, your payment is in there."

Anna rolled her eyes and sat up on her knees. She knew the drill. He had his fun with them, and then he passed out. The way he always dismissed them was telling them where he had hidden the money each time. Diamond stood up and walked naked to the drawer. Anna didn't rush behind Diamond to the dresser simply because she knew neither one of them would be keeping the thousands of dollars there.

"Have a good night, Mr. Clark," Diamond said with a big smile on her face like she'd just won the lottery.

Anna, on the other hand, didn't say a thing. Instead she looked over her shoulder at the big piece of shit for a man sprawled out on the bed. She had half a mind to go slap the hell out of the back of his head, but she knew Madame wouldn't like that very much. She was upset because she'd done a whole lot of pleasing without getting pleased. As usual Mr. Clark wasn't able to bring her to a climax and as usual he only went one round. In her life the only form of happiness she got these days were the few moments of ecstasy brought on by the constant sex.

She let the door shut behind her and followed Diamond toward the spiral staircase at the end of the hall that led upstairs to all of the girls' rooms. They passed many "hotel room" doors and heard soft moans coming from behind many of them.

"Busy night." Diamond smirked back at Anna. She saw the displeased look on her face and stopped in her tracks. Turning around suddenly and catching Anna off guard, she backed her into a wall and planted a deep kiss on Anna's lips. When she pulled away she looked deeply into Anna's eyes. "You want me to finish what he couldn't?"

Anna was at a loss for words. There she was in an empty, dimly lit hallway, naked with a woman she had sex with on a regular basis. The liquor had worn off slightly and the look that Diamond was giving her was making her feel awkward instead of turned on. Anna had been beginning to feel that the constant sex was starting to get to Diamond, because the way she'd been staring at Anna the past few weeks wasn't that of two women who just worked together. Finally snapping out of her daze, Anna turned her nose up at Diamond and pushed her forcefully away.

"Bitch, the only reason I fuck you is to survive," she sneered. "I eat your pussy because I'd rather do that than choke on my own blood. Go take Madame her money."

"No need. I'm right here."

The brisk voice surprised both of them, for neither one of them had heard her come around the corner. The air around them instantly became cold and both women's eyes shot to the floor. "Madame," they said in unison, nodding in greeting.

"My money?"

Diamond glanced up at Madame, but only for a second, before she extended her hand. Madame took a few steps forward and took the briefcase from her.

"How much is in here?" she asked sharply in a smooth voice.

"We don't know, Madame," both women spoke in unison again. "For the contents are for your eyes, and your eyes only."

Madame searched for a lie in their words and body language. When she did not find one she smiled and nodded. "Good girl," she said sweetly; but at the drop of a dime her voice changed to a cold tone. "And I mean that without the plural. Diamond, do I let anyone fuck you for free?"

Diamond's eyes began to water, already knowing what was about to happen. "N . . . no, Madame."

"Then why would you think I'd let you fuck Anna for free?"

"Madame, I—"

"Ten lashings! I will beat this fascination out of you. You will soon understand that Anna's pussy is my pussy, your pussy is my pussy, everyone's pussy is mine! Get to your room . . . now."

Diamond tried to catch her breath, not wanting a sob to come out of her mouth. She knew that if she was heard crying her lashings would for sure double. All the pleasure she'd felt moments ago was forgotten. She had tried to keep her liking of Anna under control, but it was difficult. Keeping her head bowed, she did as Madame said and went up the stairs to await her fate.

Madame knew long ago that Diamond was a lesbian and she also knew how she felt about Anna. It was obvious. That was the sole reason that Madame paired the two together. It gave her great joy to beat Diamond into submission. Breaking all of the women down mentally was what she fed off of. Breaking them down physically made her come. There was something about the torture that turned her on. Killing them though? Oh, killing them when they got out of line completed her. From the outside looking in, the normal eye would call her a pimp of women, but from the inside looking out . . . well, there was no looking out. What Madame had formed was her own women's cult. She had complete control over them all and in her own world she knew she was a god. Once she had a grasp on them none of them made it out alive . . . except one.

"Madame, I—" Anna tried to plead her case, not wanting her back sliced open like Diamond.

"Stop." Madame put her hand up. She walked slowly toward Anna, briefcase at her side, and put her hand underneath her chin. "I know you did nothing wrong. I actually came here to find you. One of your best customers has come to pay you a visit."

Anna knew that it had to be at least almost midnight on a weekday. She was used to having more than one client in a day, but only on the weekends. The surprised look on her face didn't go unnoticed by Madame.

"Oh, I'm sorry, dear. You must be worn out from Braxton." She smiled eerily at Anna. "Go upstairs and get some rest. I'll go tell Dot that he needs to request another girl. A more deserving girl."

"No!" Anna exclaimed. "I just need to freshen up a bit." She knew she never really had a choice to pass up one of Madame's clients. Not without waking up in the middle of the night to meet the grim reaper himself.

"Perfect!" Madame smiled and patted Anna's cheek. "I'll tell him to meet you in room nineteen. Oh, and tell him to ignore the screams."

Madame gave Anna an uncanny look before she turned on her heels and walked away. Anna waited until Madame rounded the corner at the end of the hall and the sound of her heels on the old wooden floor were far away before she made a move for her bedroom. Her heart was pounding in fear like it always did when she was in Madame's presence, and she rushed to do what had been asked of her.

Dot stretched out on the comfortable bed in the room he was instructed to go to. Most would be shocked to see him anywhere near a whorehouse, especially since if he wanted a whore he had a slew of them working for him; but Madame's girls were unlike any women he'd ever seen before. They were all desperately beautiful with bodies clearly sculpted by the gods. He'd been going to the place for a few years now, but had only recently become a regular. There was one woman there who satisfied every nook and cranny of his manhood and he couldn't seem to get enough of her. He traveled to that little Iowa town for one woman because in Miami he'd have to fuck ten women to get the feeling she gave him. Now was one of those times that he yearned for her touch. With everything that had taken place in his city still weighing heavy on his mind he needed his fix.

Not only had he almost gone to prison, but he'd had to bury his cousin and best friend. The last image he had of Drew was of his chest being blown apart. He was dead before he hit the concrete and seeing him sprawled out was what replayed over and over in Dot's dreams. He had men scouring for any piece of information they could find about the four people who caused so much destruction. He was so drunk with rage that he didn't want to see that even though they had a hand in Drew's death, he'd cast the first stone. If only he'd kept it an honest business deal Drew might have been lying on the bed next to him waiting for some big-booty bitch to come suck him off too. Dot didn't want to think about how he'd looked into Drew's mother's eyes and told her that he would dead the man who was responsible for her son's murder. He didn't want to tell her that the man who put a bullet in Drew's chest was the same kid Drew warned him about shortly before his life was seized. Yeah, Dot needed to get his mind off of real life for a while. And there was no better way to do so than to stick his dick inside of some wet twat.

He usually met Anna in a room called the "Naughty Room," but that night it was taken. Instead, he was in a regular-looking bedroom that had nothing but a bed, wooden dressers, and a TV on the wall. He wasn't complaining since he had just shown up without a prior appointment. He was just happy to get in and he didn't care that Anna probably just had some other man's shaft rammed inside of her. He was still going to use her as a blow-up doll and fuck until she begged him to stop. And even then he was going to keep going.

When the door opened he sat up swiftly on the bed. As usual his breath was taken away at her natural beauty. Her long hair flowed flawlessly over her golden brown shoulders. She knew he hated when she wore makeup, so her face was freshly washed; the only thing she wore was the mocha-colored lip gloss he liked. On her body she had nothing on but a black thong and a sheer black robe that was open just enough to show off her busty cleavage. She took slow steps in her open-toe four-inch heels until she got to where he sat on the edge of the bed.

"I heard you came to see me," Anna purred into his ear after she straddled him. "What is the special occasion?"

"Death," Dot told her, keeping his hands at his side. He let her do her thing; he didn't want to touch her until he absolutely couldn't stand it any longer. "I need you to help me take my mind off of some things."

"Poor baby." Anna leaned back and ran one of her hands down his face. "Tell Anna all about it, baby."

"If I talk, I just need you to listen," Dot told her and looked down at his crotch. "I like my women not talkative, but gagging."

She understood what he was saying, and she licked her luscious lips in his face. "We got all night," she said, dropping to her knees. She unzipped his pants and pulled out his thick nine inches of man. "Get it all out, baby."

At the first feel of her tongue on his tip Dot already knew that this was all the therapy he needed. He opened his mouth and began to sing his woes like a bird.

Running water was all that could be heard in Diamond's room. She'd been a good girl that night; she had kept her screams muffled. Madame hummed to herself as she rinsed the remaining blood from her fingers with the warm water streaming from the sink in Diamond's bathroom. She had just painted her nails turquoise and she didn't need the blood to dry and cake up in the crevices.

When she was done she turned the faucet off and flicked the light switch. Madame stood in the doorway of the dark bathroom and stared at Diamond's motionless body stretched out on her bed. She lay naked and completely still on her stomach. The white sheets under her were wet and a deep red. It didn't bother Madame to see her lying on a bed drenched in blood; what bothered her was that Diamond had passed out before she received her tenth lash. The gashes on her back were still leaking and if it weren't for the fact that Madame could hear her shallow breath it would have been easily presumed that the redheaded girl was dead. Madame would leave her there for a few hours. If Diamond survived, she would send in the nurse. If she didn't, her room would be up for grabs.

Madame walked to the side of the bed and brushed a curl from Diamond's sweating face. For a fraction of a second repentance threatened to enter her heart. Her light brown hand quivered slightly and she patted Diamond's cheek gently. Did she deserve to get beaten in such a barbaric manner? Staring at the girl she remembered where she found her years ago.

She had been alone knelt down by a Dumpster in the back of a bar. She was shaking in the pouring rain and looked like she hadn't had a decent meal in years. The world hadn't been kind to her, and it was apparent that she didn't have a home. Madame took her in and brought her to come stay with her and the girls. She didn't understand why Diamond would ever disobey her wishes and even think that it was okay to feel pleasure if it wasn't coming from Madame herself. The resentment in her chest soon turned to anger once again and she retracted her hand. Yes. She deserved everything that she got. She was ungrateful. She stepped away from the bed and walked through the darkness of the room to the door.

"Good night, Diamond," Madame whispered before she shut the door behind her.

Checking the golden watch on her wrist, she walked down the hall of the upstairs of her inn. The inn was her greatest accomplishment in life. The upper portion of it was dedicated to her girls. Once you got up the spiral staircase there was a big black door with a keypad instead of a doorknob. In order to get past the door you had to know the code; otherwise, there would be no entry granted. Behind the door was where the girls' quarters were and nobody but them was allowed up there.

She opened that heavy door and made her way back down the spiral staircase to make her rounds on the bottom level. Most of the rooms upstairs were empty because most of the girls were finishing their jobs downstairs, and when she passed each closed door she smiled at the sounds coming from the other side of them. After passing the final door she decided to take a stop in the kitchen to make sure her hired chef was there preparing breakfast for the next morning. Her guests paid good money to stay there and partake in the extra activities they provided; the least she could do was make sure they were well fed. All she had to do was peek in the kitchen to see that everything there was good. The muscular chef, Vonzell, smiled when he saw her beautiful and flawless face.

"Looking good, Madame," he said and licked his lips at her. In front of him he was mincing fruits for the fruit salad on the morning's menu. "If you want I can clear off this table and mince you with my tongue."

Madame gave a small chuckle and bit her lower lip. She'd had Vonzell before and, although he pleased her from the front way and the back, she would rather go to her room and pleasure herself. "A great offer, baby," Madame said. "But I was just making sure things were okay for the morning. But seeing that you didn't even need me to check in on you, I'll have Brandy come and satisfy that big bulge in your pants."

She left before he could reply, and she made her way to her room, the biggest room besides the dining room in the whole inn. It was on the lower portion of the inn and at the foot of the longest hallway. Her heels clicked feverishly on the wooden floor and when she got to her door she placed her palm where the doorknob should have been. There was no code to punch in; the only way to get past that threshold was with her fingerprints. She heard a small hum followed by a click, and she pushed the door open.

"Finally. Peace," she said to herself and kicked her shoes off.

As a little girl she had always dreamt of being a princess, except that was the furthest thing from what she was. Her mother had left her father when she was just a toddler. He was an abusive and controlling man. She was no better, though. She was addicted to beauty and, sadly for Madame, that was all she cared about. She didn't care that she had a growing daughter who needed her; she didn't care that the nights when men took her to lavish restaurants her daughter was at home starving. She didn't even care that when she was asleep in the room down the hall the men she brought home would fondle Madame's growing woman parts.

When she couldn't take it anymore Madame moved in with her father in hopes of living a better life. That proved to be a fantasy as well. From the moment she stepped foot in his home she was getting slapped around. Whenever something didn't go right in his life he hurt his only daughter while his new wife watched. Why did they do it? His wife helped because when he was beating his daughter it kept his hands off of her and her children. She constantly was coming up with new forms of torture for Madame and that went on for years, until Madame slit their throats in their sleep when she was eighteen.

All she wanted to do was live like a princess and the people who had the power to give her that lifestyle were selfish and evil: two traits she'd gotten from them and manifested into something that no one would see coming. When she was done with her father, stepmother, and stepsiblings, she went back for her mother. With her she wanted to feel the life drain from her, so she wrapped her hands around her neck as she held her underwater in the bathtub.

Yes, the inn was her greatest accomplishment. It once belonged to her stepmother's father, but when she died and her children weren't there to make a claim to it she was the only one there to receive the keys. She turned it into something better than anyone ever imagined and made sure her room was the equivalent of a queen's room in medieval times, complete all the way down to the weapons hanging from the walls and a royal throne.

But she didn't stop there. She had a huge building but nobody to live there with her. She began recruiting young women who reminded her of herself. They had no one to turn to, and nowhere to go. They were all weak when she found them and she built them up, only so she could break them down and build them up again. She saved them all and in return they pledged their lives to her and her sick, twisted ways. She controlled them. She was their god. All of their pictures hung on a wall in her room, staring down lovingly at her bed. Now she could wake up feeling loved every day.

After she showered, she draped her body in silk and prepared to get in bed. She clapped her hands twice so that the lights would dim but not shut all the way off. Lying back she tried to get comfortable in her soft bed but right before she closed her eyes she heard a soft knocking at her door. With a raised brow she stood back up, feeling the softness of her red carpet on her toes, and walked to the door.

"Anna? What is it that you want?"

Anna tightened her hand around the wad of cash in her hand, daring not to drop a single bill to the ground. She hadn't been invited inside of the room so she just extended her hand.

"My night's earnings, Madame."

Madame's piercing brown eyes narrowed at Anna, making her feel like she was nothing more than the lint floating around in the air. Madame was dressed in her nightclothes and Anna hoped she wouldn't be punished for interrupting her sleep. Hopefully, the money would be enough to save her from a lashing. She held her breath and focused her eyes on the ground until she felt Madame remove the money from her hand.

"Thank you," Madame said and turned her back on Anna to take the money to her vanity dresser. She heard Anna make a move to leave, but she had one more question to ask. "Anna, why did Dot come to see you tonight? It was very unusual, especially since he didn't call before he came. Did he . . . contact you somehow?"

Anna feared that Madame might have thought that she and Dot had a conversation outside of the inn, and she swallowed hard. The last thing she needed was for the person who held her life in her hands to think she was sneaking around behind her back.

She shook her head feverishly. "No, Madame. I would never sneak to use the phone without permission." Anna was so flustered she commenced blabbering about her whole night. Madame's back was still toward her and she feared what might happen when she turned around. "He said he came to see me tonight because he was distraught. He was telling me about somebody named Quinton and how he's responsible for his cousin's murder."

Madame turned around and glared so murderously at Anna that she flinched and dropped to her knees.

"I'm sorry, Madame! I shouldn't be talking. I'm sorry!" Anna covered her head with her hands and arms.

Madame stared at the girl shaking literally at her feet, but it felt as if she was looking through her.

No. It can't be after all these years.

"You are dismissed," she whispered. "Leave now!"

Anna didn't need to be told again. She stood up and wrapped the robe she was wearing tighter around her waist before running, literally, away.

Madame's breath was rigid and she put a hand to her chest. So many memories were coming back to her.

Memories that made her think of her one failure. The one failure that she thought of every day, and the reason why her grip on her girls was so strong. Disloyalty had caused her to lose the opportunity of a lifetime.

She went to lie back down without even bothering to count the money Anna gave her. It proved pointless because Anna's voice kept playing through her head. After about five minutes Madame knew that she wasn't going to get any sleep with an unsettled mind. She stood and prepared to go pay one of her guests a visit. *For his sake, he better hope that what he said was just an innocent coincidence.*

Chapter 7

The worst feeling in the world is having to choose between myself and somebody I love. It's like if I choose them, I'm going to be unhappy every day of my life. But if I choose me it feels like I'm not being loyal to somebody I know would go to hell and back for me.

Rhonnie sighed and set her journal to the side of her, placing the pen on top. She was a fighter so she didn't let the slight ache in her arm bother her when she placed her hand back in her lap. For the most part the gunshot wound had healed up pretty nicely. If it hadn't been for her dad's quick thinking she would have bled out in the back seat. Painfully, but successfully, he was able to get the bullet out without causing any further damage. The patch work he did was also pretty decent; it lasted until they got back to Nebraska and she was able to receive proper medical attention.

Always the hardheaded one out of the two sisters, Rhonnie of course didn't listen to the discharge instructions that were sent home with her. She was too independent to have to depend on anyone to do anything for her. After the second week of being in a sling and getting pissed off at the fact that she was too limited, she figured it was time to put her arm back to use. It hurt like hell but she started off easy with simple stretches. She then eased herself into lifting weights until finally her arm was strong enough to be used without a sling.

Being shot made her realize that she had taken many things in life for granted. Being able to do things like write in her journal had become something to be thankful for. Simply because if that shooter's aim had been on point that day, her shoulder could have easily been her heart. She realized then, in the moment she was flying backward with her eyes on the clouds, that she wasn't ready to die. What had she really seen in life, or done, that she really wanted to? When she first agreed to do what her father had asked of them years ago, it was because she could see past it. They would get in, make some money, and get out. Now it was like she couldn't make it to the other side.

Quinton had indeed saved his daughter's life, but he brought her back with a different mindset. She knew what a great dad Quinton was, and she knew that she was a great asset to him; but she was ready to be a great asset to herself. And hopefully he understood. She sighed and shook her head because putting her thoughts on paper was usually enough; this time it wasn't. The only thing that would make her feel better would be to call him and tell him how she felt. She had enough money saved up to walk away from that life and figure out what she really wanted to do. It was time to pursue other things.

She picked up her phone to call him but surprisingly she saw the word Dad along with the picture for his contact already displaying on her screen.

"Hello?"

Brayland had been given the job to look after Rhonnie and Ahli, but the key was to not let them know he was there. After arriving in Omaha, Nebraska, Quinton surprised Brayland by giving him $25,000 and his Chevy Avalanche.

"Now, you can either take this money and run with it, or you can stay here and work for more," Quinton had told him.

The money was greatly appreciated but Brayland knew that in two months it would be gone. He was used to living a lifestyle where money was something that always came in. It would be hard to break the bad habits he had picked up in the last few years. When he went to the mall he usually left with more than $10,000 worth of things. He knew that it would be in his best interest to stay where he could make some change, at least until he moved on to bigger and better things.

His car was parked about fifty feet from where the pearl white Lexus was parked outside of the Oakview mall. He had been waiting almost an hour for Ahli to return to it, and she must have been on a mission. She stepped out of the mall with what looked like ten bags. In order to get that kind of shopping done in under an hour she had to know exactly what she was going in there to get.

Brayland smirked to himself unknowingly, because everything about Ahli was calculated. She was always on point with everything she did and it intrigued him. That, along with the fact that she was sexy and thick as hell. Those were the main things that made it hard for him to stay away. When she opened her mouth to speak he had to tell his dick to *stay down, boy*. She had a voice that would do numbers on a sex hotline. Nothing that came out of her mouth was worthless to listen to. If he had to be completely honest he would come upfront and say that the only reason he had chosen to stay back was because of her. After meeting her and seeing the type of things she did, he had to stick around. If anything happened to her it wouldn't be under his watch.

The smile left his face as soon as he realized it was there. He waited for Ahli to throw her bags into her back seat and get into the front seat before he started his own engine. For a truck, the engine purred softly. He waited to pull off until Ahli had pulled far enough ahead of him that the tail wouldn't be obvious. When she left the mall's parking lot he already knew where she was going just because she turned right instead of left. She thought it was her own secret place, but little did she know Quinton knew all about the apartment that she kept a secret from everyone, including Rhonnie. However, Quinton felt it was best to at least let her think she had the place all to herself.

He followed her until finally they reached the destination, where she pulled into her garage and he parked in a vacant parking spot. He watched her like a lion watches its prey and his eyes couldn't help but caress the way her body filled out her Chanel short sweat suit. His eyes lingered on her cleavage and he was mesmerized by the way her breasts bounced with every step that she took.

Knowing he wouldn't be able to see her once she made it through the secured entry of her apartment complex, Brayland hopped out of his car. She had already made it into the building by the time he hit the entrance but, lucky for him, just as he approached the door a couple was making their way out.

"There you go, my man," the man said and held the door open for Brayland.

"Good looking," Brayland said and smiled kindly at them so that he didn't look too suspicious.

"No problem!" the man said, grabbing his brunette girlfriend's hand and making his exit with her.

It was the first time Brayland had actually been inside of the building, so he didn't actually know which way to go. Usually he just stayed in the car for a little while until it was time for him to leave and check on Rhonnie. This time, though, he knew that Rhonnie was safe and sound back at the house, so he had a little more time on his hands.

He didn't want to guess on the doors so instead he followed the scent of the Dolce & Gabbana perfume that was lingering in the air. Doing that led him to an apartment door on the third floor where the scent was the strongest. He reached and grabbed the golden doorknob, twisted it easily, and pushed the black door open.

"'I like the way you move and the way you do your thing.'"

He heard the sounds of a soft, pretty voice singing a song that he was too familiar with. He followed the voice to the kitchen of the apartment. There he saw the shopping bags thrown on top of the dining room table and Ahli bent down in the kitchen, putting something under the sink.

"I always liked the theme song to *Cousin Skeeter* too," he said loud enough to get Ahli's attention.

Startled, Ahli stood straight up and whipped around, wishing that her purse weren't so far away from her. Seeing that it was only Brayland, her guard went down slightly. She nonchalantly looked him up and down, taking in his fly-boy image. "What are you doing here, Brayland?"

"You know you really shouldn't leave your door open like that. Anybody could come up in here."

"You mean like you? And how did you know how to find me anyway?"

"Uhh . . ." Brayland fumbled with an answer, because no matter what he said it would blow his cover.

"Mm-hmm, just like I thought," Ahli said, sighing and rolling her eyes. "My dad got you watching Rhonnie and me, huh? Figures. He don't know how to just let us be sometimes!"

"He just being a man and doing what a dad does," Brayland said, trying to come to Quinton's defense. "I never had a dad to do shit for me; be thankful."

"I am thankful," Ahli said. "But I'm also grown and should be able to wipe my ass without a pair of eyes on me."

"Ay." Brayland threw his hands up. "I might follow you around, but I don't want to see nothing that comes out of your shit chute."

A laugh weaseled its way through Ahli's lips and it caught her off guard. She tried to cover her mouth with her hand but it was too late; she was cracking up by then. "I hate you," she said and playfully swatted his arm.

"No, you don't," Brayland said and leaned against a cabinet in the kitchen. "Especially not once you get to know me."

Ahli rolled her eyes at him again and turned her nose up. "We can be cool," she said, using her foot to close the cupboard behind her. "But I don't think I would ever know you."

"Why is that?"

"Because I wouldn't allow myself to."

"Why not? I'm a good dude."

"I never said you weren't."

"Aw, I get it." Brayland took a few steps closer to Ahli and put two fingers to his chin. "Let me read you right quick. Hmmm, let's see. You fell in love awhile back with a nigga you thought you would be with forever. It didn't work out. You got your heart broke. What? He stopped calling or something? You realized he never really loved you the way he said he did?"

Ahli clenched her jaw and swallowed. Her brown eyes traced Brayland's face, and she instantly got agitated at the smug smirk on his face. She was trying to figure out what he thought was so funny.

"If somebody you loved tried to make you choose between them and more people you loved, what would you do? That is the hardest decision to ever have to make, but when I did make the decision he couldn't understand it. So yes, he did stop calling. And yes, I did realize that he never really loved me the way he said he did. But that has nothing to do with why I won't allow myself to really know you."

Her response was so terse that it took Brayland completely left. He stood before her awkwardly, not knowing what to say, so he just dropped the subject. Out of the two sisters it was apparent that Ahli was the more guarded. She never said too much, just enough to make a point. For the most part she was able to keep Rhonnie in check and make sure that everything was perfect for her father's business. Still, there was something about her that made him want to crack the surface. He had learned a long time ago that nothing was as it seemed. And even though Ahli seemed like a put-together woman, he wanted to know what the ingredients to the glue were that held everything together.

"I guess the cat is out of the bag, huh?" Brayland said.

"Huh?"

"Your secret crib." He moved his hands in a motion that let Ahli know that he was talking about her apartment.

He walked into the living room like he owned the place and Ahli smirked at his boldness. She followed him and shrugged her shoulders, looking around her spacious two-bedroom apartment. The walls were so white that when the sun touched them they looked golden. Her carpets were tan and were so soft walking on them could be mistaken for walking on clouds. Her furniture was subtle, but sexy. She had a deep red wine couch and love seat, with a large brown mahogany coffee table on top of an eccentric African rug. On the walls hung many different paintings, all with people of African descent in different scenes. Where one would assume that a TV would be hanging on the wall, there was a piano instead. On top of the piano there was incense burning, and the blinds to the patio were wide open. The whole room always gave her a positive vibe and brought good thoughts to her mind. It was what she called her "Room of Peace."

"I figured that if he didn't know about it by now, he would find out eventually. He has never let Rhonnie and me stray too far from home. This is my spot but I don't even live here. Crazy, right?"

"A little bit," Brayland said, walking around the living room and eyeing all of the paintings. The room was giving him the most soothing vibe he had ever felt in his entire life. When he reached the piano he ran his fingers along the top of it before he opened it up and sat down on the stool.

"Don't . . ." Ahli tried to stop him from touching her mother's old piano but she stopped at the sound of the first keystroke.

Brayland's fingers graced the piano almost like they were one with the keys. Soon the whole apartment was filled with the sweet melody from the sheet of music propped up in front of him. He glanced up at it every so often, and it shocked her how beautifully he played. What blew her away and made her take a seat was when the man before her started singing the lyrics to Lauryn Hill's song "Ex-Factor" in a twisted, but beautiful, mash up.

"'See no one loves you more than me/And no one ever will/No matter how I think we grow/You always seem to let me know/It ain't workin'.'"

"'It ain't workin'.'" Ahli closed her eyes as she sang the adlibs to the song, much like she used to do with her mother.

"'And when I try to walk away . . .'"

"'You'd hurt yourself to make me stay . . .'"

"'This is crazy,'" they finished in unison.

Brayland stopped playing and smiled at his fingers. It had been awhile since he played the piano. He had grown up and become accustomed to playing with guns.

"Who taught you how to play and sing like that?"

"Nobody," Brayland said, closing the piano and standing.

"Somebody had to." Ahli studied his face and took notice of how he was trying to make a quick getaway. "Need I remind you that you barged into my shit without being invited and put your raggedy hands on my mother's piano? The least you can do is answer my question."

Brayland sat back down on the piano stool. That time he faced Ahli. He chuckled at the determined look on her face; and, the way her forehead was wrinkled, he knew it might be in his best interest to answer her questions. "Has anybody ever told you how cute you are when you're mad?"

"Boy, don't you even try it!" Ahli said, clenching her teeth so that she wouldn't smile. "Now spill."

"My grandmother," Brayland finally admitted. He smiled thinking of the old woman who had raised him from a boy to a man. "After my mother left my dad and me, I would go to her house after school. She kind of forced the piano on me at first, telling me that one day I would thank her for teaching me how to use my fingers so graciously." He paused and chuckled. "My mom wasn't shit, but my granny? She was determined to give me a good life. She ain't want the streets to take hold of me so she kept me in the house and taught me how to play every instrument she knew how to."

"She seems like a pretty stand-up woman. How did you end up in the streets?"

"She died," Brayland said, staring at the palms of his hands. "When I was sixteen. And my dad passed not too long after that. It was unexpected and she never had the chance to put her estate in my name and not my mom's. That cheating ho sold all my granny's shit, including the house and the cars. Left me on the streets while she lived like a queen in some white man's palace. So I had to do what I had to do."

"Brayland, I'm so sorry," Ahli said, not knowing what else to say. She understood then why he didn't have any issue with relocating to Nebraska. There was nothing in Miami for him, nothing good anyway.

"What you sayin' sorry for?" Brayland looked deeply in her eyes. "It ain't your fault. It's just life. This game ain't as pretty as these pictures you got on your wall."

It was Ahli's turn to look at her palms. She just nodded, not knowing what to say but still not ready for him to leave yet. She tried with all of her might to think of another question to ask him, but failed.

"How did you learn how to sing? All the dust on this piano and the fact that it needs tuning lets me know you probably haven't used it in a while."

Well, that wasn't what she wanted to talk about, but she had already dodged one of his questions already. "When I was little," Ahli started, "like seven or eight, Rhonnie used to get these really bad nightmares. And I told my mom that I didn't like to hear my little sister cry, so I asked her to teach me how to play her piano. That melody you just played is the melody she taught me. So every night, until Rhonnie stopped having nightmares, I would put her to sleep in our old living room on the couch. I would make up a different song every night, and it worked like a charm every time."

"I can tell that you really love your sister." Brayland nodded. "And even though she talks a lot of shit I know she loves you too."

"Yeah," Ahli said and blinked away the tears in her eyes. "When our mom died we went through pretty hard times. Our father had been in some pretty big trouble with the law for a few things so he couldn't provide for us the way he used to. He didn't have access to any of her money. Thousands and thousands of dollars, just gone. For a while I had to be the woman of the house."

Brayland felt like he was scratching the surface and he didn't want her to stop talking. He wanted to know everything about her that she would be willing to tell. "How did you get into doing what you're doing now?"

"Remember when I told you that my dad had been in trouble with the law?" Brayland nodded. "Well, it wasn't any petty crimes. My father was once one of the most wanted burglars in Chicago. He used to hit high security banks and houses, empty them dry, and leave without a trace. He went to prison for it, but didn't have to serve his full sentence because the witness suddenly didn't know exactly what happened. When he came home my mother handled all the bills. We were able to still live nicely, but when she died we were equivalent to beggars. We had to eat somehow so my daddy taught Rhonnie and me everything he knew about high-profile robbery."

"Robbery? How did you end up in Miami sellin' drugs then?"

"My daddy's friend, Lance, always sets up our hits. He sent us to a house where I guess the Last Kings had set up shop in the city. Rhonnie and I thought we were snatching money bags. Turned out to be cocaine."

"Yo, y'all really robbed the Last Kings?"

"Yeah," Ahli said, confused by the incredulous look on his face. "Why did you say it like that?"

"Because." Brayland shook his head still in shock. "Just know you a cold piece for that shit."

"It wasn't harder than any of our other hits. They need to tighten up their security. Anyways, that's the shortened version of how we got to where we are now."

"One more question."

"Shoot?"

"What's Ma's name?"

"Rhebecca." Ahli sighed. "But lately it's starting to feel like that's all I know about her."

Her facial expression grew distant. Brayland sensed that he had touched a sensitive spot and once again he backed off. He awkwardly rubbed his hands on the legs of his white-washed jeans and glanced down at his white and red Air Max 90s.

"I think I'm gonna dip out and grab a bite to eat," he finally said. "Plus, I appreciate Q letting me crash at y'all spot and all, but it's time for me to find a place of my own to lay my head."

He stood to leave and made his way back to the front door. His palm had just wrapped around the knob when he heard Ahli call his name.

"Brayland!" Ahli said again, hoping he hadn't left just yet.

"What's up, Lee?" Brayland said, stepping back into the living room area. He checked his pockets and looked to where he had been sitting. "Did I leave something?"

"No. I just have one more question. How many times have you followed me here?"

"Like four or five," he answered honestly.

"Well, why'd you come in today?"

After a few moments of looking into each other's eyes Brayland finally just licked his lips and smiled to himself. "You're the coldest girl I've ever met in my life, Ahli," he said, his baritone voice low. "I like to listen to you speak even if we ain't really talking about shit. You're like one of them mysteries in them white people shows and I just want to crack you. You ain't scared to do what you gotta do to survive; you ain't scared to shoot a pistol. But I done been around bitches like that before, and you're just different. You're deep. I can tell that by just being in this one room, and I like that about you."

"That sounds like a bunch of game." Ahli stood up and tried to walk around Brayland to show him back to the door.

"I don't sing for just anybody," Brayland said, stopping her in her tracks and bringing her in front of him.

"You were singing about love. You don't love me, Brayland," Ahli whispered up at him. "Plus, this is a new place for you. New women, new pussy."

"But I could love you. I already know that I like you," he responded smoothly and moved a loose curl from her face. "And I don't know none of these bitches here. I've been too busy watching you. And wanting your pussy."

He couldn't help himself. He placed his arms around her waist, pulling her closer to him. He then placed a gentle kiss on her forehead, but when he tried to kiss the tip of her nose she grabbed the back of his head, forcing their soft lips to meet. The two shared a powerful kiss, neither one wanting to come up for air.

Ahli forgot all about her ex, what's his name, because in that moment it was all about how good Brayland was making her feel. His hands rummaged her body like she was a lost and found and he was looking for his possessions. He unzipped her jacket and tried to lift her cami over her head. She shook her head and looked into his eyes. "Rip it. The bra, too."

Her demanding stature along with the sexiness of her voice made his thick shaft stand at full attention. He did what he was told and when he saw her breasts jiggle he almost did the same to her shorts and panties. Tossing the ripped clothing to the side he knelt his head down to taste her nipples, something he often wished he could do.

Now he was doing it and they tasted better than he could have ever imagined.

"Mmmm, Brayland," Ahli moaned into the air and tried to slip her hand into her pants. His tongue felt so good and her throbbing clit was begging to be touched.

"Hell nah." Brayland grabbed her hand and threw it back. "This all me right now. You ain't even gotta do all that."

Ahli bit her lip and took a step back, giving him the perfect view of her perky nipples. "Mmm," she said, sucking her teeth. "Is that right?"

She didn't give him a chance to answer; instead, she started to walk slowly toward the master bedroom. When she was halfway there she glanced over her shoulder and into his lustful eyes. There was something about him that made her want every inch of him, literally. The way he had kissed her had her feeling something deep in the pit of her stomach and she didn't want the feeling to go away. Forget making love; she was going to let him hit it however he wanted. She needed it. She slowly bent over, while pulling her shorts and panties down to the ground, and never broke eye contact with him.

"Damn, girl," he said when he was staring at a perfectly round ass. He cocked his head so that he could see her fat pussy lips smiling at him.

She giggled, standing back up and kicking the clothes off of her feet. She rubbed her breasts and switched the rest of the way to the room, making her cheeks jiggle more than usual. When Brayland finally entered the room he saw that she'd already assumed the first position. Face down, ass up.

"Like that?" he asked and took his shirt off, revealing his completely tattooed chest and muscular torso. "A'ight. Just know you can't get rid of me after this." He kicked his own shoes off and dropped his pants.

"Who said I would want t . . . Ahhh!"

Her words got lost in translation when Brayland swiftly gripped her lower back and entered her with a powerful stroke from behind. "You what?" Brayland asked and thrust again.

Every sensation had awakened in Ahli's body and she buried her face in her pillows. Brayland began to give it to her so good from behind that her toes curled and she forgot what his real name was. Right then he was simply "daddy." He was telling the truth when he said that this was "all him." The only sounds that could be heard were her pleasured screams of submission.

"Who you giving this pussy to, Ahli?" Brayland asked with his face twisted up in pleasure. The sight of his shaft slipping in and out of her curvy body was enough to drive him crazy. She was so beautiful and the sweat dripping from her body, the wet smacks coming from her love box, and every sound escaping her mouth let him know he was getting the job done. A job he knew now that he could never let another man have. "I said who you fucking, Ahli?"

"Nobody," Ahli whined into the pillow. "Nobody, daddy. Please don't stop."

"I won't if you promise me this is mine. This my pussy, girl?"

"Yesssss! Oh my God. Yes!"

Ahli's body quivered violently and Brayland couldn't hold his nut any longer either. He pulled out and released himself all over her spine. The two climaxed in unison and collapsed on the bed in each other's arms. Ahli looked into Brayland's handsome face in wonder, letting her fingers glide over his sweaty forehead.

"That wasn't supposed to happen," Brayland said.

"Yes, it was." Ahli smiled. "If not now, someday."

The two shared another deep kiss, only to be cut short by the sound of Ahli's phone vibrating from the kitchen.

"I gotta go get that," she said and got up on shaky legs. "It might be Rhonnie."

She knew how ridiculous she looked trying to walk to get to her phone, and she swore she heard a snicker. Smiling like a schoolgirl she was finally able to make it to where she'd left her phone on her dining room table. She moved the shopping bags out of the way and saw her father's contact on the screen.

"Shit," she said to herself and tried to clear her throat. "Hello?"

"I need you back home ASAP."

"What's going on, Da . . ." She stopped, realizing she had just called another man that less than ten minutes ago. She cleared her throat again and finished. "Umm, what's going on, Dad?"

"Just get here. Rhonnie is already here. We're just waiting on you. I tried to call Brayland; if you talk to him tell him to come too." The tone of his voice let her know that whatever it was had to be serious.

"Okay. I'll be there in half an hour." She disconnected the call and walked back to her room.

"That was my dad. We gotta go," she said to Brayland who looked like he was on the verge of going to sleep. "Business as usual."

It had been almost a month since the episode in Miami and Rhonnie had healed up quite nicely from being shot. Quinton never said it, but that was one of the most petrifying moments of his life. Losing Rhebecca after everything they'd been through was already hard, but losing his baby girl would have ripped him to shreds. He thought that things would go back to normal after, but Rhonnie had been noticeably distant from everyone. She wasn't her usual feisty self and was seemingly nonchalant about everything.

Quinton understood. Nothing about the Miami trip had gone as planned. He thought they would all be sitting with $50,000 more each in their bank accounts, but that was not the case at all. Brayland had changed that, although Quinton was not complaining. The boy had saved all of their lives, after all. For that, Quinton saw it fit to split the earnings evenly across the board. He knew that with what Brayland had done, there was no way that he could reside in Miami safely anymore. There would for sure be a price on his head and Quinton figured the least he could do was offer the boy a fresh start. Nebraska wasn't Miami but Quinton was positive that Omaha would give the kid as much of the city life as he needed.

Now, though, Quinton was facing a dilemma. This last job was supposed to put him and the girls in the position to live seemingly normal lives. He felt like a selfish man for continuously putting his daughters in the line of fire, but with all of their cuts shortened he knew he couldn't be done just yet. That was the only reason he ended up answering Lance's phone call.

"What's going on, Lance?" Quinton answered his cell phone dryly. He sat on the balcony that was connected to his bedroom, puffing a Cuban cigar. He wore nothing but a pair of shorts, a tan bucket hat, and a pair of sunglasses, letting his muscles brandish in the sunlight. His bedroom faced the back of the house, and the view was a calming one. Every house in the neighborhood had something special about it; one even had a small pond. His eyes fell on the golf course in the distance and he waited for Lance to answer.

"Nothing much, man," Lance responded in a rushed tone. "Just tryin'a see how you're living. I heard about what happened down in Miami. Bruh, I swear on my mother that if I knew that nigga was on foul play like that I would have never sent you."

Quinton listened to his boy speak, trying to find the sincerity in his voice. "Aw, yeah?" Quinton ashed the cigar in the ashtray on the small, round table beside him. "How'd you hear about Miami?"

"Nigga, everybody knows about Miami. Dot called me a little bit after it happened trying to get information about you and the girls."

"What did you tell him?"

"What do you mean what did I tell him?" Lance sounded genuinely insulted. "I told that nigga this was my first time working with y'all too. And that I ain't have too much information on you. I also told that nigga if he wasn't on that snake shit none of this would have happened and his mans would still be breathing."

Quinton wanted to be angry with Lance, but he knew he couldn't. Lance had trusted the game just like he had done and they both knew that was a big mistake. The game changed every day, and integrity wasn't one of its finest lessons anymore. After a few moments of silence Quinton finally sighed into the phone. "Everything is everything, my man. I can't fault you for another man's greed."

"That's love. How is Rhonnie? I heard she got clipped by one of Dot's shooters."

"She's good now." Quinton raised an eyebrow. "How'd you know it was her who got hit?"

"What I've learned about those girls of yours is that Ahli is the brains and Rhonnie is the brawn. If anybody got shot, it would be her. "

The two men shared a laugh because they both knew how true the statement was. Quinton stopped laughing abruptly and looked at the cigar burning slowly between his fingers.

"That was the scariest moment of my life, man. At least with Rhebecca I knew it was coming. That's my baby girl. If anything ever happened to her, I'd—"

"I'm already knowing, big homie, trust."

"Shit got me thinking about leaving this shit alone, you feel me? I got the house and the cars but . . ."

"But what?"

"There's still something I need to do. And I still need a couple more zeros in my bank account."

"I'm glad you just said that, man." Lance paused to cough. "I got the package you sent me and I understand why it was shorter than what we discussed, given the bad deal and all. But that still doesn't make up for the fact that it was short. I got a family to feed too, you feel me? Tiffany is going off to college and this shit is hitting my pockets something crucial."

"So what you saying?"

"I got the plug on a job not too far from you in Coralville, Iowa. A five million dollar house and the councilman who owns it is taking his family out of town this upcoming weekend. Inside scoop is he only keeps half of his riches in the bank; the other half is inside of a vault in his cellar."

"How much we talking?"

"Seven hundred thousand. Maybe more."

Quinton sat up straight in his chair when he heard the figure. With that kind of money he would be straight for a lifetime. "How do you know all of this? And if he has that kind of money in his home I can only imagine the measures he's gone through to secure that it stays there."

"Most men with that kind of money aren't good people," Lance said and chuckled. "He's not a mob boss; the only things that keep his security there are their paychecks. If something happens to their job with him, they can get another elsewhere. I have some inside guys and they have already sent me a blueprint of the entire house; they even have the numbers to the vault. The cameras are run all together off a computer system and I have a buddy who can hack into it so that you can get in and out with no problem."

"What's the catch?"

"You have to get the job done on their shift; otherwise, the window of opportunity is gone."

"How many people know about this?"

"You mean now? Just you, me, the two guards, and my computer tech guy."

"How can you trust the guards?"

"We know their home addresses, where their wives work, and where their children go to school. Need I say more?"

Quinton nodded and thought about the proposal. This was more up his alley. He knew how to use a gun, but he was used to not having to brandish one. Before he opened his mouth to give Lance an answer he already had an answer. He was in.

"I have to talk to the girls about it first. But in the meantime send me over the details and the blueprint of the house. No more bullshit."

"Never," Lance said. "And, Q? If you decide your answer is yes, just be careful."

Lance disconnected the call before Quinton could say another word. Behind him in his bedroom Quinton heard his computer ping. He put his cigar out and left it outside in the ashtray so that he could go back inside of the house. He sat at his computer desk and sure enough when he opened his e-mail he had all the information he needed about the hit. He knew for a fact how sufficient Lance's computer guy was; he had been the one to set Quinton up with an untraceable e-mail address. Quinton scrolled through all of the details of it and got the contact information for the two guards, the date and time for the hit, and most importantly the vault numbers. The only thing that put a damper in any plan was when he saw the date and something clicked in his head. It was the same day as his next meeting with his probation officer.

She was cool, but not that cool. The last thing he could risk was going back to jail for missing a thirty-minute meeting.

"Shit," he said to himself.

The only way that he would be able to be a part of the hit would be if he sent Rhonnie and Ahli in his place. Which had never been a problem before, but he knew that the Miami incident was still fresh for them. Especially for Rhonnie. He just hoped that her love for money would trump her memory and she too would see the bigger picture. One last job and $500,000 spoke volumes for them all. In the end everybody would eat and with that kind of money no smile on their face would be fake again.

He knew both Rhonnie and Ahli were out of the house so he went back out to the balcony to get his phone. He placed phone calls to Ahli, Rhonnie, and Brayland to meet at his house ASAP. It turned out that Rhonnie was still in the house so he wouldn't have to wait for her. Ahli, on the other hand, said she was on the other side of town and it would take her about thirty minutes to get home. Brayland didn't answer his phone, but Ahli said that she would try to reach him herself.

He pressed END on the last phone call and then sat down to finish off his cigar before he made his final proposition. He could only guess how the meeting was going to go and, of course, he was right.

"Hell no!"

"Rhonnie, just lis—"

"No, Ahli! The last job Lance set us up with we stole drugs from notorious drug kingpins and I got shot! Hell nah. Ding! Try again."

Rhonnie sat on the living room couch next to Brayland with her arms folded across her chest. Ahli sat on the floor to the right of the coffee table with her knees pulled up to her chest and Quinton sat in a big chair facing them all. He just laid down the complete details of the hit, showing them the blueprints and safe numbers. Just like he thought, Rhonnie blew up as soon as he stopped talking. Except he didn't think she would go as hard as she did.

"This is seven hundred thousand dollars we're talking about, Rhonnie! And it's just doing what we're good at." Ahli was trying to reason with her sister because she wanted to do the job, but she wouldn't do it if Rhonnie wasn't on board. Yes, she was sure that Brayland would be down to do it, but he wasn't trained like Rhonnie. He didn't know her like the back of his hand like her sister did.

"Fuck that money." Rhonnie stared at her father with fire in her eyes. "Daddy, I love you, but I'm out. That's the reason why I came to this meeting. I would let you tell us more about the job, but I don't even want to waste your time like that."

"What about the money?" Brayland finally spoke up. "I could use that kind of dough."

Rhonnie didn't budge. "What *about* the money? Y'all can still go. I'm all right when it comes to the money department. I have a lot saved up in a couple of accounts that will hold me over until I decide what I want to do. I'm tired of robbing people and killing people. That shit shouldn't be normal! But it's normal to me and that's crazy." She paused and sighed deeply. "Daddy, I know you've always done what you always thought was best for us, and because of you I have more money than most. But did you ever think that maybe we only do this for you? Have you ever taken a step back and thought about what we want?"

"Every day."

"Then why you still got us out here moving like trained assassins? Other dads treat their daughters like princesses. You treat us like some fucking sic 'em dogs! I almost died in your arms and you still want to send me on another mission. What kind of man are you?"

"Rhonnie, that's enough!" Ahli stood and Rhonnie did the same.

"You know I'm right, Ahli! I ain't doing this fuckin' job. He can do the shit by himself or with you two."

"I can't do this without you, NaNa, you know that."

"Well, I guess today is the day you retire too, then."

Rhonnie glared at her father one more time before storming out of the living room. Shortly after, they all heard the front door slam.

"Daddy, I—" Ahli tried to apologize for Rhonnie's behavior but Quinton held up a hand to stop her. He'd since changed into a Jordan sweat suit and he sat in his chair looking relaxed and comfortable. His face held no expression and his eyes focused on the rug on the floor. Rhonnie's words were circling in his head.

"Your sister is right," Quinton said in a low voice. "I've been so focused on money when I should have been focused on you two. We have more than enough money to sit on for a while. I guess I just never want fall into the pit again; enough money just hasn't been enough money for me."

He cleared his throat and finally looked up at Ahli. Ahli, the one who resembled her mother, almost like a spitting image. He smiled at her and cleared his throat. "I'm going to call Lance and tell him that the deal is off."

"But, Daddy, that's a lot of money. I can talk NaNa into going."

"But you won't have to," Quinton said and turned to Brayland. "Son, give me and my daughter a second. Go on to the basement and pour us up some drinks. I'll be down in a second. I need a hit of something strong."

"Yup," Brayland said, getting up so that he could leave the two of them alone.

When he was gone Quinton turned back to Ahli, taking in what a beautiful and strong woman she had become. Rhonnie was right; he'd been viewing them as his shooters and not his daughters for some time now. He'd missed out on so much of what was right in his face. He was too busy trying to be unselfish that he ended up being selfish anyway. He had taken their lives from them and that was not at all what Rhebecca would have wanted. She wanted them to have something she only tasted for a short while: freedom.

"I think it's time," he finally said after staring at her for a while.

"Time for what?"

"That I tell you a little bit more about your mother." Quinton stood up and headed to the stairs. "Follow me."

Ahli didn't let a foot get between her and her father as she walked up the steps with him. With all of the mystery surrounding who her mother really was, she wouldn't let the opportunity pass to know who Rhebecca was. She totally forgot all about Rhonnie's blowout argument when she walked into Quinton's master bedroom. She took a seat on his bed and he sat in the chair at his computer desk. Quinton stared into Ahli's eyes for a long time, taking her in piece by piece. Everyone said she favored him, but he knew that was a lie. She was the spitting image of Rhebecca. A constant reminder of what a beautiful and great woman she once was.

"Have I ever told you the story of how I met your mother?"

"No," Ahli said. "You both just used to tell me it was love at first sight. That's it."

"Yes." Quinton smiled sadly, thinking about the day he met Rhebecca. "Indeed it was. But I think it's time for you to know the full story."

Ding!

The sound of the bell at the front desk got the attention of a very attractive front desk worker. She turned around and found herself face to face with a young man with a promising face. Looking him up and down, she noticed that the shirt and jeans he wore were drenched from the rain outside and he was carrying a small travel bag with him. By looking at him you would think he was just a man down on his luck, not a deadly thief.

"Oh, no, and here I am thinking that the rain had stopped."

"No, it's still going." The man offered a kind smile to her. "Just started pouring actually. It got so bad that I couldn't see the roads anymore."

"Where were you headed?"

"Home," the man answered simply. "I'm just looking for a place to lay my head for the night until I can start moving again in the morning. This was the only place open."

The woman smoothed her hands down her skirt suit outfit with her eyes still on the man. She slowed her hands when she reached her hips, causing his eyes to shift downward.

Damn. Baby is stacked. *He hadn't noticed how thick the woman was until then, and on top of that she had the face to match. He quickly averted his eyes back up and glanced at her nametag.* "So uhh, Tamia? Do you have any rooms available?"

"Let me check." Tamia went over to her computer and began to tap away at the keyboard. "May I have your name please?"

"Quinton Jacobs," he said, giving her a fake last name. "And I will be paying with cash."

"No problem, Mr. Jacobs. Just give me one second."

While she looked for an available room Quinton used that time to take a look around the large inn. The décor was very antique like; everything looked fragile. Like the stuff your grandmother would slap you for just looking at when you were a child. It had white walls and a spotless white carpet. The lobby of the inn had many gold chairs to sit in, completed with a stone water fountain and stacks of magazines on the many tables. He found it slightly odd to have such a classy place in the middle of nowhere, but he was grateful to have found something before it got too late in the night. He would have never made it to the next town in the storm if he'd have kept driving. Still, something told him that if they were able to take a cash payment to give it to them.

"Okay," Tamia spoke again. "This is one of our busiest nights but we do have a room available. It's one we don't use very often since its one of our"—she cleared her throat—"regular rooms."

"I'll take it," Quinton said quickly. He was so tired he just wanted to lie down in a comfortable bed. "Are there bugs?"

Tamia looked at Quinton as if he were a bug. "The Opulent Inn doesn't have bugs," she said, not sounding too fond of his joke. She activated a room key and handed it to him. "That will be one hundred and fifty dollars for the night. Breakfast is served in the morning until eleven o'clock. Your room number is fifty-eight. It is down that far hallway and you will take your first right. Continue down that hallway and it will be on your right side."

When he walked away Tamia was slightly disappointed that he didn't glance back at her. The more she had looked at him the sexier he got. She could see his muscles in his wet T-shirt and she wondered what his arms looked like when they flexed. Yeah, she definitely wouldn't mind taking a quick break to be broken off by that. Little did she know, a pair of round breasts and a fat backside made his manhood rise, but it would take more than that to make him bite the bait.

Quinton followed her directions until he reached a hallway with wooden floors. He turned the corners he'd been instructed to turn and was glad when he finally found the room at the end of one of the many hallways. The coldness of the inn was starting to get to him since, after all, he was soaking wet.

He put his key against the door until he heard it click and he pushed it open. The first things he noticed about the room was that it smelled fresh, like the laundry had just come back. And also the fact that the light was already switched on. He figured that maybe someone had hurried to place brand new sheets on the bed.

The room was decorated much like the rest of the hotel. There were beautiful paintings hanging from the wall, clean tan carpet, a flat-screen TV, and a queen-sized bed in the middle of the room. He walked past the closed bathroom door and tossed his bag on the bed. The only thing he could think about was how good it was going to feel to have some hot shower water hitting his face.

He searched for the remote to the television and found it by the lamp on the nightstand by the bed. Turning the TV on, he flicked through the channels until he found a movie that he wouldn't mind watching when he got out of the bathroom. Just when he was about to turn the volume up on the TV he heard a thud, like someone had dropped something, not too far away from him. He muted the TV and stood still so that he could hear around him better. After about thirty seconds he didn't hear anything else. He pointed the remote back to the TV.

"What the hell is that?" he said to himself and listened to the room. When he didn't hear anything else he shook his head. "Must have been one of the other guests."

The words had only been out of his mouth for a few moments when he heard a whimper. That time he knew he wasn't being crazy; the sound came directly from the bathroom.

He turned the TV back up before he reached in his bag to grab the fully loaded chrome 9 mm pistol from it. Slowly, with the gun aimed, he walked to where he was sure the sound came from. He was a fool to get a room at an inn in the middle of nowhere; he'd seen all those scary movies.

Placing his ear on the cold white door he tried to listen for something on the other side of it. Sure enough, he heard rapid breathing. Someone was in there. He aimed the gun and wrapped his free hand around the door-knob. Twisting it, he flung the door open and extended the weapon in front of him.

"Don't move!" he called out with his finger itching on the trigger.

What he saw was not what he expected at all. The bright lights above the wide mirror were on, shining light on the bloody scene before him. There was deep red blood all over the sink and counter with drippings that led all the way to tub. He thought that it would be someone in the room trying to pull the okie-doke and rob him. Instead, he found a trembling young woman, in her early or mid-twenties, sitting on her knees in the middle of the floor. She looked distressed and like she was caught red-handed in the middle of committing a crime. It was evident by the blood trails that she had been in the middle of frantically trying to rinse the blood from her body. Her hair was disheveled, but he noticed that she was wearing makeup and she was wearing an expensive silk robe with lingerie under it.

"Shh," she said, not moved by the gun. Her eyes were wide and they darted around him to the entrance to the room. "Shhh. P . . . please. Don't let anyone hear you." There was a terrified look frozen on her face and she looked around him to see if anyone had come in the room with him.

"Who are you? How did you get in here?" Quinton asked and glanced around for the weapon she'd used to cut herself just in case she tried to use it on him.

The woman at the desk must have double booked the room, and whatever was taking place right then he knew he wasn't supposed to see. The woman just stared at him as if she hadn't heard the questions. When he didn't see a weapon he knelt down to his knees too, staining his pants at the knees. Why? He didn't know. He should have just turned around, grabbed his bag, and asked for another room. But, the way she looked, the fear-stricken look on her face, and the eerie feeling in the room made it impossible for him to walk away. He couldn't leave her like that.

"Why are you cutting yourself?" he asked.

The woman looked at her hands, the floor, and the tub before finally looking back at Quinton. Tears appeared in the corners of her doe-shaped eyes and she took an unsteady breath, shaking her head. "This . . . this isn't my blood."

The intensity in the room magnified with her words and Quinton felt the hairs on the back of his neck stand up. Quinton didn't have time to process her words when he heard the whimpering coming from behind her. It sounded like a baby cry and when he looked over her shoulder he saw just that. There was a small brown sleeping baby wrapped up cozily in one of the white bathroom towels. Well, it used to be white; now there were bloody handprints all over it.

What has she done? *Quinton asked himself.* "Did you kill his parents?"

"Did Madame send you to find me?" *She ignored his question and asked her own. She searched his face through fearful eyes knowing that if his answer was yes her plan would be foiled.* "Did you tell her about the baby?"

Quinton had no idea what she was talking about. "Listen, I just came to this place to get some sleep before I head out again in the morning. I didn't expect to find a woman drenched in blood with a baby in my bathroom. I'm just hoping that if you killed somebody that the body ain't in here too."

She didn't say anything; she just examined his face until she felt like he was telling the truth. She turned away from him and grabbed the red-stained bar soap that she had been using before she heard the hotel room door open. Turning her back on him she leaned over the tub so she could scrub vigorously at her hands and arms. She wanted to hurry up before her baby woke up hungry and screaming. That was the last thing she needed.

"You should leave," *she said over her shoulder.* "If Madame finds you in here with me she will make me kill you too."

"Don't worry about me. I can handle myself. I'm more intrigued by you. Are you going to tell me who you killed?" *Quinton asked again.* "Was it his parents?"

"Her," *she corrected him. Although she was slightly comforted by the fact that he was not one of Madame's henchmen, she knew that she didn't have much time before her absence was noticed. Her heart was pounding and, no matter how badly she tried to, she couldn't stop the shaking of her body.* "And yes. I killed her father. I'm her mother."

He noticed the rush in her motions. She was moving like a person who had somewhere to be, or someone who was about to run.

"Here, let me help you," he said, tucking his gun away when she got quiet. The only sounds coming from the room were running water and the TV. He reached for her and she flinched when he removed the bloody robe from her body. "I'm not going to hurt you. I've bodied a couple of people in my day too. I ain't have anybody help me get rid of the blood, though."

From where he knelt on the hard floor Quinton noticed that she had many healed scars on her back. The kind of scars that only came from deep gashes. "You don't have any blood on your lingerie or legs but we need to rinse this shit off of your body before you get an infection." Quinton helped her wash the blood from her arms and hands. When finally the last of the pink was being washed down the drain he asked, "What's your name?"

The woman looked curiously at him, trying to figure out if she should trust him. Of course she couldn't trust him; she didn't know anything about him. Yet, he surprisingly wasn't unnerved at the scene at hand, and he also hadn't run to get help. He was a mystery to her. Where had he come from? Why had he been booked in her secret hideaway room? Nobody was ever booked there; she was sure that most of the other girls in Madame's inn didn't even know it existed.

She dried her arms and hands off with a towel before wrapping it around her body. She grabbed another clean towel from under the sink and scooped her baby up into it. She continued to ignore the man in the room with her and stood so that she could continue with her plan, but he stood too. He blocked the doorway and wouldn't let her pass him. She sighed and glared at him.

"Tamia," she answered with a lie.

"*Nah, try again. I just met Tamia at the front desk.*"

She cut her eyes at him and clenched her teeth, pondering if she should tell him her real name. "*Rhebecca,*" she unwillingly said. She didn't have much time and he was getting in her way, literally. She brushed past him holding the baby tenderly to her chest. "*You?*"

"*Quinton.*"

"*Well, excuse me, Quinton. I'll be out of your hair shortly.*"

She set the baby down on the bed and ran back into the bathroom, reaching under the sink once more for the bottle of bleach that was there. There was so much blood in the bathroom, but she wanted to get rid of all the evidence proving that she'd been there. Since it was so fresh it came right up, but it took awhile to get it all clean. The bathroom was spotless by the time she was done, but there was one more place with blood that she had to get rid of.

"*Do you have a change of clothes?*" she asked, surprising Quinton, who had been watching her clean the bathroom better than any housekeeper. She noticed the puzzled look on his face and pointed to the blood on his still-damp clothes. "*I need to dump those on my way out.*"

"*Yeah,*" he said, looking down at himself, pleased at her keen eyes. "*Let me get up out of these before the people come after me for a dead nigga I don't even know.*"

He turned his back on her, walked back to the bed and, forgetting that there was a sleeping baby there, he plopped down. The baby felt the sudden movement and began to whine in her sleep.

"*Shh, shhh.*" Rhebecca rushed to soothe the cranky baby. "*It's okay, baby. Mommy won't ever leave you alone again. I promise.*" She held the baby like she was as fragile as glass when she rocked her back to a comfortable sleep. Quinton saw the love in her eyes and felt it seeping from her into the small body she held.

"I'm not trying to be in your business too much. I've learned in situations like this the less you know the better. But by the amount of blood that was in the bathroom one can only assume it was drawn by a knife. Usually if a woman kills her boyfriend it's something quick, like a gunshot to the chest or head. So, I have to know, why did you kill her father?"

Quinton removed a pair of shorts and another T-shirt from his bag while Rhebecca laid her daughter between the pillows again. He didn't want to put the clean clothes on his dirty body, and he also didn't want to risk taking a shower while she was there. He opted to just take his shirt and jeans off and sit on the bed in his Calvin Klein boxers. He handed her the clothes, which she took, and then she knelt down to look under the bed, holding the clothes to her stomach. He waited patiently as she extended her free arm under and brought it back, clenching the handle of a briefcase in her fist.

The contents inside of it was what was going to save her. Everything she had been planning had fallen upon that very moment and the last thing she ever expected was for Quinton to impose. She reached under the bed again and that time brought back a plastic bag containing two outfits: one for her, and one for her baby. She removed the towel from her body and put on a black T-shirt, a pair of dark blue jeans, and a pair of black flats. She sighed after she put the footed onesie on her baby, careful not to upset her, finally ready to answer his question.

"He wasn't my boyfriend. And I killed him because I had to," she whispered, stuffing the bloody towels and clothing into the plastic bag. "I didn't have a choice."

"Did he have a gun to your head?"

"No."

"A knife?"

"No."

"Did he try to kill you?"

"No."

"Then why would you kill the father of your child? Are you a sociopath?" He studied her face. Neither her wild hair nor the dried mascara on her face took away from her natural beauty. After a few moments of him staring intently into her eyes, she looked away.

"Madame," she whispered and set her daughter back down. *"She makes us do horrible things for her, and if we don't comply she will do unimaginable things to us. She made me do it. She made me kill him."*

"Why?" Quinton leaned on the wall behind him, trying to make sense of her words.

"Because she is evil. This is the Opulent Inn, the place to fill all of your heart's desires."

"My heart's desires?"

"Yes. If you couldn't tell by my original getup, I am what people call a whore. I . . . we are all sex slaves." Rhebecca gazed into space as she spoke. *"Me and all the other girls. We all belong to Madame."*

"Others? I only saw one other girl. "

"Because we are completely booked up tonight. Very wealthy men travel from all around the world to spend their nights with Madame's girls. Prosecutors all the way down to drug lords, like Lorenz, my daughter's father."

Suddenly he remembered that Tamia had called the room he was booked in a *"regular"* room. Now he understood why. *"So this is a brothel?"*

"Worse. More like a cult."

"So this Madame person, why did she make you kill the father of your child?"

Rhebecca looked down at her hands and breathed deeply with quivering lips. A few tears fell from her *eyes, but she wiped them away when she felt them on her cheeks. "When our guests come," she started, "they tell us things they never tell anyone else. Because we never leave this place. So they confide in us. Many of us have regular customers. Lorenz is . . . was one of mine. He is"—she stopped and cleared her throat before correcting herself again—"was a big drug dealer in Texas. He didn't even know he fathered my child. Babies aren't allowed here. I had to keep it a secret."*

"How?"

"Well," Rhebecca said and smiled at her sleeping Mini-Me, "it helped that my stomach was small the whole nine months. The girls here can volunteer to sleep with the patrons, or do Madame's bidding."

"Kill for her," Quinton clarified for himself.

"Yes. I don't know for sure all of Madame's business dealings. This inn is only one of them. She is a cruel woman. She used some of us to seduce her enemies and then others to kill them. I had to. It was the only way I could wear baggier clothing to hide my stomach closer to my baby's birth date. When the time came, I passed my labor off as the flu. No one wanted to come near me."

"Is her father one of Madame's enemies?"

"No, not until I gave her more information than she needed to know."

"What do you mean?"

Instead of answering him directly with words, she grabbed the suitcase that she'd taken from under the bed. "The last time he was here, Lorenz was so drunk after we got done, you know, that he told me things he wasn't supposed to." She opened up the briefcase and took out a small Baggie with a substance that Quinton had never seen before. She then pulled out a sheet of paper with fine writing on it.

"What is this?" Quinton asked when she handed him the paper. He studied the formula written on it and felt his eyes grow wide at the treasure he was holding in his hand. He grabbed the small Baggie from her, too, and studied the contents. "Did he . . ."

"Yes." Rhebecca swallowed. "He created a new drug. And she wants it. She told me to slit his throat from ear to ear, and watch him bleed out to make sure he died."

"Well, that explains the blood." Quinton reached to put the paper and bag back in the briefcase, but when he grabbed it he was hit with another surprise. "What's this?"

In the briefcase there was enough money to make the job that he was coming on look like child's play.

"My savior," Rhebecca said and once again stared in Quinton's eyes. "I was supposed to be dropping off this paper to her safe before I cleaned up, but instead I robbed it. I'm the only one who knew the numbers to the safe. She trusted me more than the other girls. She can't get this drug. She will force us all to take it and she will sell it. If she sells it she will get even more money and be able to buy a bigger facility. I wouldn't wish this hell on my worst enemy. I can't stay here anymore. I made the decision tonight that I have to run. My daughter, she's getting louder and she's begun to move around. If Madame finds her she won't hesitate. She will kill her. I have to run. I only have another thirty minutes before one of the girls does inspections. I need to be gone before then."

Quinton saw the tears streaming from her eyes, but even more so he saw the terror there again. His hand, with a mind of its own, found its way to her soft brown cheek. He stroked it with his thumb. "I would ask you how you ended up here," Quinton said in a low voice, "but I can tell in your eyes that you don't want to remember that part of your life. Did this Madame put those gashes on your body?"

"Yes." Rhebecca nodded. "She punishes us with a machete. Please help me. I'll give you money. I just need you to drive me far away from here."

Quinton's brow furrowed again. He was deep in thought. A part of his brain was yelling for him to turn the girl in and keep the contents of the briefcase. A bigger part was telling him to help her. Never in his life had he seen anything like what he was witnessing in front of him. His eyes went to the sleeping baby and he felt something in his chest that he never had before. She was little, so innocent. She deserved a chance at life. He didn't know if his decision was made because his own mother hadn't fought for his life the way Rhebecca fought for her daughter's. Or if it was because, even looking as distraught as she did, she was the most beautiful woman he had ever laid eyes on.

"Okay," Quinton finally said after pondering over it for a little longer. "I will help you."

"Really?" Rhebecca threw her arms around him before jumping to her feet. "We have to go before Madame wakes up!"

He grabbed her arm before she got too ahead of herself and he brought her back down on the bed. He shook his head at her when he saw her bewildered expression.

"I thought you said you were going to get me out of here."

"I am," he said, letting her arm go. "But if Madame is as ruthless as you say, and if she really has a crew of killer hoes running around, going straight out of that door wouldn't be a smart idea. What time does she get up in the morning?"

"Eleven o'clock. Every morning."

"What would you do to save your daughter's life?"

"Anything."

"Would you die?"

"Ten times."

"Good. Go to your room. Leave the baby and the brief-case with me. I'm leaving at ten o'clock. If you want to get out of here, you'll be there. I'm driving an all-black Impala, the only one out in the parking lot."

"What? No!" Rhebecca looked from Quinton to her baby. *"That's . . . no! How do I know you won't rob me? I don't know how I'm going to get out if—"*

"Do you have another plan? If I wanted to rob you I would have put a bullet in your forehead and given your kid to the wolves. Trust me."

Rhebecca clenched her teeth so hard that for a second Quinton thought she was going to take the baby and the briefcase and bolt out of the door. Her movement was so sudden that he didn't even have time to flinch. She placed both hands on his cheeks and put her face so close to his that she could smell the steak he had for lunch on his breath.

"Promise me you won't leave me." Her voice cracked and he could feel every shake coming from her hands.

He put his hands over hers and awkwardly rubbed them with his thumbs. *"If you are at my car by ten o'clock, I promise I won't leave you. Now go to your room before your absence is noticed."*

Slowly Rhebecca let her hands drop to her lap. Sighing deeply she turned her body so that she could pick her daughter up and hug her sleeping body. She listened to the quick little breaths and felt the beating of her little heart. She smiled sadly into the baby's shoulder. She never thought that she would be able to love anybody the way she loved that little girl. She had given her something that had gone away a long time ago: the will to live.

"I love you," Rhebecca whispered before handing the baby to Quinton. "She likes to be held when she sleeps. When she wakes up there is milk in a bottle hidden in the nightstand next to the bed. Please keep her safe."

She stood and walked reluctantly to the door. Leaving her baby behind that time was the hardest ever, but something was telling her that she could trust Quinton now. It seemed like an entire lifetime since she looked in someone's face and didn't see any lies. She was comforted by the fact that even if she wasn't able to make it away from Madame's clutches, her baby would have the opportunity to really live. And she would know that her mother loved her.

"Wait!" Rhebecca was halfway out of the door when Quinton called out to her.

"Yes?"

"What's her name?"

In a perfect world the image she turned and was looking at was one she thought she would wake up and see when she had her own family. Rhebecca smiled at Quinton rocking the baby on his bare chest, holding her like she could shatter any second.

"Ahli. Her name is Ahli."

Reliving the moment he met Rhebecca brought goose bumps to the back of Quinton's arms. Mentally he remembered the complete story, but verbally he told Ahli everything except the part about her. He would never tell her that biologically he was not her father because regardless of that she was his child. After spending just one night with her as a baby he knew he could never let the world get to her. The way her small hand wrapped around his finger foreshadowed how she would always have him wrapped around hers. Waking up to her wide eyes, exactly like her mother's, studying his face quietly signified that she trusted the unknown person. She smiled a wide, toothless smile at him as soon as she saw he was awake and went into a sea of babbles. He knew then at that very moment what the feeling in his chest had been love.

"What happened when you got away?" Ahli asked.

"She asked me to take her somewhere safe and where no one would ever find her," Quinton said, thinking about the two-hour drive back home.

"Where did you take her?"

"To my house. I like to say I fell in love with her on my way back to Nebraska. Her mind was one I knew I'd never come across again. Once she came into my life, she never left until God called her home."

Ahli sat feeling like a revelation had overcome her. So many things began to make sense now; the dots were connecting. Knowing her mother's past allowed her some insight about why they did the things they did, in the way that they did them. She sighed, thinking that Rhebecca was a slave at the age that she was now. It was something unimaginable. Her body wasn't even her body, her mind wasn't her mind.

"What happened to the formula she found? Did you guys sell it?"

"We tossed it the first chance we got," Quinton answered without batting an eye. "A drug like that is worth billions, and if you think the war on drugs is bad now, it would have been disastrous and influenced many wars. If it had hit the streets, whoever had it in their possession would be king of many lands."

Ahli studied her father's face not knowing if she should believe him. She decided that she didn't want to press the matter right then. Instead, she rose to her feet and advanced on him so she could throw her arms around his neck.

"Okay, King Arthur," she joked in his neck. "I love you, Daddy. You're everybody's hero."

He hugged her tightly back until she withdrew from him and he patted her cheek. "I love you too, LaLa. Your mother would have been proud of you. You're strong like her."

"I hope so."

"I know so." Quinton stood up and sighed. "Go on and check on your sister so I can tell Lance that we're going to sit this job, and every other job, out. It's time for us to start living our lives honestly. Starting now."

"Okay," Ahli said. "I'll have her call you when I'm done chewing her ass out. I love you!"

"I love you too," Quinton said again.

When she left he ran his hands down his face and chuckled to himself. After he sent Lance the message saying that he was out, he readied himself to go downstairs to the basement and hit the bar with Brayland. Before he left his room his eyes rose to the ceiling, although it felt like he was looking past it. He shook his head.

"You always said these girls would be the best and the worst of us combined." His voice was hushed, but he knew she could hear him. "You were right. As always."

Chapter 8

Night had fallen by the time Ahli finally caught up to her sister. There were only a few places that she could have been. The first place she checked was the downtown bumpy slides, a place both of the girls found refuge in as kids. With some waxed paper and a ripped cardboard box they felt like superheroes gliding down the slides at what seemed like the speed of light. When she didn't find her there she knew there was only one other place she could be. Ahli finally found her at an old park that their parents used to take them to when they were younger.

The creaking of the old swing interrupted the quiet around them. Rhonnie had her back to her as she swung low back and forth. Her hair was free from its ponytail and flowed freely in the wind with every swing. Ahli stood silently a few feet away on the pavement until Rhonnie slowed the swing. "I wondered how long it would take for you to find me."

"I should have come here first," Ahli said, walking up on her sister and taking a seat on the swing next to her. "I thought you would be at The Slides though."

"Nah," Rhonnie said, still looking straight ahead. "I didn't have much of an appetite."

"I guess there is a first for everything, right?" Ahli said, her voice bitter. She eyed Rhonnie's side profile and shook her head. "You know you're wrong, right?"

"Yup."

"You don't care?"

"Nope."

Ahli closed her eyes and took a deep breath to keep herself from slapping her sister in the back of her head and knocking her off the swing. The smugness sprawled all over her face was making Ahli's insides boil. Times like that it was hard to be the older sister. She wanted to fight her sister like she was a random chick off of the street.

"Listen, Rhonnie," Ahli started, trying to keep her voice even. If Rhonnie said something out of turn she knew that she wouldn't hesitate to lay hands on her. "I don't give a fuck about how you feel toward Daddy right now, or the fact that you want your freedom. If I ever hear you talk to my father like that again I will beat the dog shit out of you."

Rhonnie was shocked at first. Her sister had never talked to her like that before. Quickly regaining her composure, she turned to her sister with her lip turned up. She was about to open her mouth to get smart but Ahli gave her a deathly stare.

"Say something stupid and I'ma take off on you." Ahli threw in the towel on keeping herself collected. "By disrespecting my father you disrespected me. Despite how you feel now about the jobs we've done, understand you still did them. Understand that you weren't complaining back then, or when you were sitting your ass up in Gucci buying up the fucking store. So don't you dare patronize my father about the things he has done to ensure that we are okay! Bitch! You got me fucked up!"

Rhonnie jumped to her feet and stared down beseechingly at her sister. "You. Aren't. My. Mother."

She tried to walk away toward where her car was parked, but Ahli grabbed her arm with a grip so strong she would have had to use pliers to free it. Ahli snatched her back and also stood. She blocked Rhonnie's path and squeezed Rhonnie's cheeks tightly with her right hand.

"I never said I was, but walk away from me and I'll whoop your ass like I am." Ahli pulled Rhonnie so close to her that their noses were touching. "We are all we have, Rhonnie, and I'll break your ankles before I let you walk away from me, do you understand?"

Rhonnie breathed heavily with an angry, wrinkled forehead. Her hands had balled into fists and she wanted nothing more than to swing on her sister. However, she knew that was one fight that she would lose. Whereas Rhonnie excelled in gunplay, Ahli had hands for days. Those were bruises that she could do without. Also, angry and all, the level of respect she had for her sister would never allow her to lay a hand on her.

"I said, do you understand?"

"Yes!" Rhonnie said and snatched her face away from her sister's iron grip. "Now get the fuck off me!" Defeated, she plopped back down on the swing. She folded her arms like she used to when she was little and didn't get her way.

If Ahli weren't so mad she would have laughed at the sight of her little sister pouting. "He told Uncle Lance that we aren't going to do the job," she told Rhonnie and watched the astonished expression wash over her face. "He said starting today we're going to start living right. Like, how did you put it? 'Normal people.'"

"Really? He turned down all that money?"

"Yes, because he loves you more than any dollar amount." Ahli looked down at Rhonnie like she might have been the dumbest person she knew. She pulled her phone from her back pocket and tossed it. "Stupid. Now call him, apologize, and tell him that you love him so we can go eat. I'm starving."

Rhonnie caught it; and she wanted to say something else to her sister, but Ahli was already walking to where she'd parked next to her car. She rolled her eyes and stared down at the phone for a few seconds, not knowing how she was going to start the conversation.

"I'm sorry, Dad," she practiced, and cleared her throat and tried again. "I'm sorry, Father." She giggled to herself nervously at how ridiculous she sounded. Never had she talked to her father in the way that she did before she stormed out, so she was wary of what his response would be. She pressed his contact in Ahli's phone and placed it to her ear.

He answered after the second ring and didn't give her the opportunity to speak. "What's up, Rhonnie?"

"How did you know it was me?" she asked since she was calling from Ahli's phone.

"Father's intuition," he said. "Ahli always shoots a text before she calls."

Rhonnie couldn't read his mood by his voice. She tried to talk but got tongue-tied. She felt like shit. Ahli was right; no matter what, Quinton hadn't deserved for her to go off on him like that. She had just been in the heat of the moment with clouded judgment.

"Daddy, I—"

"Never apologize for how you feel," Quinton said. "I will always love you, no matter what, you hear me? Plus, you got that hotheaded attitude from me. You boil quick and come down slow every time."

"I'm still sorry." Rhonnie had a lump in her throat. "I didn't mean to yell at you like that. I feel horrible."

"It is I who should feel horrible. It's been past due for us to leave this shit alone. I guess I thought the three of us were invincible. What happened in Miami was a real eye-opener for me. The things you said were exactly what I needed to hear. I've been so focused on giving you life that I've been taking it at the same time. You were right and I want to give you girls your freedom back. You have enough money to figure out your own paths. On one condition, though."

"What's that?"

"You stay at home. Until some nappy-headed boy sweeps you off your ashy-ass feet."

Rhonnie giggled and she heard her dad chuckle too. She felt relief come over her and she smiled into the phone, nodding. "You got yourself a deal, old man. I love you, Daddy."

"To the moon and back." In Quinton's background the doorbell sounded. "That's probably Brayland. He just stepped out and probably forgot something. I'm about to just make his drunk ass stay here."

"Okay, Daddy." Rhonnie laughed again, picturing a usually put-together Brayland stumbling around. "Handle that. Me and LaLa are about to go grab some food. I'll see you later."

She kissed the phone and hung up when he said goodbye. She tried her best to put her mean face back on when she marched up to Ahli's car.

"Here." She tossed the phone through the driver's side window. She pulled her car keys out of her pocket and unlocked the doors to her gray BMW M3.

"Girl, stop. I heard you over there laughing."

"Whatever," Rhonnie said, standing on her own driver's side and looking at Ahli through her window. "I don't know why you think you're somebody's mama. Bitch gets some dick and starts acting like she runs the world."

"What?" Ahli leaned out the window with wide eyes but Rhonnie was already in her car cracking up.

"You must think I'm dumb!" Rhonnie rolled her passenger's side window down so Ahli could still hear her. "I know you and Brayland have a thing going on! Anyways, follow me!"

She started her car and drove off, leaving Ahli no other choice but to follow the BMW. Ahli wanted to know exactly how her sister knew about Brayland, because the deed hadn't even been done for a full twenty-four hours yet.

Is it that obvious? she thought with a cheesy smile spreading across her face.

"So how was it?"

Ahli continued eating her pizza and texting on her phone, pretending like she hadn't heard Rhonnie's question. She felt her sister's eyes boring a hole in her forehead but she still didn't look up. The smile threatened to spread across her face, but she fought the urge.

"I know you hear me! I see the corners of your mouth twitching, you want to smile so bad! Now spill! Before I hop over the booth table and choke it out of you."

"I don't know what you're talking about."

After leaving the park they decided to go eat at a family-owned pizza restaurant called La Torro's. Their family recipes were amazing and both girls loved going there to get their fill of cheesy goodness. That night the restaurant didn't have too much traffic, but that was the way the girls liked it. Having a father like theirs, they'd naturally become cautious of large crowds. The red and white tiled floor of the restaurant accented the black booth seats and red tables nicely. It was a smaller establishment, with only about fifteen tables, but that didn't take away from its popularity. The aroma in the air was mixed with fresh dough baking and the huge pepperoni pizza in front of them.

"I know you, LaLa. You like that boy. And if he ain't hit it yet I'm sure he's going to in the near future. Shit, if you don't, I might bend over backward for him one time."

"I'll beat your ass!" Ahli exclaimed just like Rhonnie had hoped.

"Aha! I knew it! You let him hit it! Ohhh my God, the cobweb queen finally got some diz-ny-ee!"

"Ahhh!" Ahli squealed through her hysterical laughter. She flicked a string of cheese in her sister's direction. "Why would you say it like that?"

"Because it's true! You've been touching on yourself since that ugly boy left for college." Rhonnie put her hand up stopping Ahli's protest. "Stop. That nigga was ugly as hell, don't lie. Brayland is definitely an upgrade."

Ahli rolled her eyes but secretly agreed. She thought back to the moments of intimacy she shared with Brayland. By the way they tussled around the bed and how he sensually stroked her inside and out, she knew that this was only the beginning of their journey. Or so she hoped.

"He's a'ight I guess." She bit her lip, smiling.

"A'ight my ass," Rhonnie said.

"Whatever." Ahli looked slyly at her sister's eager face. She rolled her eyes. "Yes, okay. He hit this shit so good that I want to do it again, you happy?"

"Yes!" Rhonnie clapped her hands. "Now maybe you won't be so uptight!"

Ahli took a big bite of her pizza and made a face. She suddenly was thinking maybe she should have hit Rhonnie back at the park. Maybe some sense would have been knocked into that girl.

The two continued talking the way they always did. One conversation led to the next, which led to the next, until they Ahli felt someone walk up behind her.

"Damn, y'all done ate up most of the pizza!"

Turning around in her seat she looked up and saw Brayland grinning down at her. The lowness of his eyes was a dead giveaway that he was a little tipsy, but he seemed to be well put together still. She scooted over so that he could take a seat next to her and the two of them gave each other bedroom eyes for a few moments.

"Mm-hmm," Rhonnie said and made a loud slurping sound while drinking the last of her drink. "Y'all ain't slick."

"I don't know what you're talking about, shorty." Brayland winked at her while grabbing a slice of pizza. "But what I do know is that I'm hungry as hell. Your dad had me at the crib drinking gin and juice and shit."

"He was trying to get you fucked up." Ahli made a face thinking about how gin tasted going down. "He could have at least poured you up some Hen."

"Nah, it was cool. You see, we men"—he patted on his chest—"can handle anything. You feel me?"

They all shared another laugh. Rhonnie put her elbow on the table and leaned her head on her palm. "You got here fast." She playfully batted her eyes at him. "You like my sister that much that you would speed through traffic just to get to this pizza spot?"

"Nah, I was just cruising over there on Ninetieth when Ahli hit my line sayin' y'all was here."

Ahli nudged him with her shoulder, scrunching her face up at the man who was sending her stomach into a fit of butterflies. "Oh, so you ain't speed over here?"

He went to say something to her; but something he said wasn't sitting right with Rhonnie. Her forehead wrinkled in confusion and she leaned back in her seat, removing her arm from the table so she could point at him.

"Ninetieth? I was just on the phone with my dad not too long ago and he said you came back to the house. He thought you forgot something."

It was Brayland's turn to look taken aback. "Nah, I left a little while after Ahli did," he said, trying to understand the look on her face. "I wasn't going to head back that way until y'all did."

"No, no, no." Rhonnie shook her head. "I heard the doorbell ring when he was on the phone."

The butterflies that were in her stomach just seconds before died slowly one by one with every word Ahli heard Rhonnie speak. The expression on Rhonnie's face reflected the slow dread building up in her stomach.

"You sure you heard a doorbell, Rhonnie?" Ahli asked, hoping her sister would clarify.

"Yes, Ahli. Loud and clear. He said he thought it was you, Brayland. He thought you might have forgotten something."

"Nah, it wasn't me," Brayland told her. "What's up with y'all faces, though? Quinton can't have company?"

"My dad never has company," Ahli responded.

"And the only people who know where we live are sitting at this table right now."

No more words needed to be said. Brayland pulled a fifty dollar bill from his pocket and threw it on the table and the three of them jetted out of the restaurant. Rhonnie couldn't shake the bad feeling that she had in her gut as she weaved in and out of the traffic on the interstate. Something wasn't right and she could feel it.

The thirty-minute drive to their house was cut down to twenty and she was the first to pull up. She parked her car in the driveway but didn't bother to turn it off or shut her door behind her when she hopped out. She heard Ahli and Brayland pull up as she was running full speed to the front door. She knew once she saw the door wasn't even all the way shut that she shouldn't go in the house, but she pushed it open anyway.

All the lights in the house were on, which was odd because although he had the money to pay the lights up for ten years, he still lived like they were in that one-bedroom apartment. If you weren't using it, turn it off, was his motto.

"Daddy!" she yelled, running through the foyer of the home. "Daddy!"

She checked the kitchen first and when she didn't find him there she went to the living room. She would wish for the rest of her life that she hadn't stepped foot in that room.

"Nooooooo!" Her bloodcurdling scream could be heard from a mile away. Tears instantly came to her eyes. "Ahhhhhhh!"

Her gut feeling at the restaurant had been right. She had just stepped foot in and was witnessing the aftermath of a massacre. She indeed had found her father; he was sitting in his favorite chair. Except he didn't hear her calling for him, and he never would again. The blood that was splattered all over the walls and floor made sure of that. She knew it was his blood because his shirt was completely stained from being stabbed multiple times, and he wasn't just slit ear to ear. His entire throat was missing.

"Rhonnie, what's wr . . . ahhhhhhhh! Nooooooo!" Ahli had followed her sister's screams only to join them with her own. "Daddy! Oh my God, Daddy. Not my daddy!"

Brayland walked in and as soon as he saw the bloody living room he pulled the pistol from his waist and took off the safety. He went around the house to search for the intruder but it was clear that they were long gone. When he came back to the living room he told them that the house was clear, but he wasn't sure if they heard him. Both women were on the ground, clinging to each other like their lives depended on it. Both of their bodies convulsed violently as they cried into each other's shoulders.

"Damn," Brayland said, scratching his head and letting the hand holding the gun fall at his side. Whoever had done this to Quinton made sure he died painfully. The deep red blood splattered everywhere was enough for him; he didn't want to see where his throat had been thrown. "Who got to you, man?"

Although she felt like her entire soul had been ripped from her body, Ahli knew that they couldn't stay there. She tried to pull away from her sister but Rhonnie had her in too tight of a bear hug, so instead she placed her lips by her ear.

"R . . . Rhonnie," she whispered tearfully. She clenched her eyes shut and tried to ignore the odor coming from her father's dead body. "Rhonnie, we have to go. We have to get away from here. Go to the artillery room in Daddy's bedroom and get all the weapons you can carry, okay?"

Ahli felt her sister shudder in her arms and she wanted nothing more than to comfort her forever, but she couldn't. She pried herself out of Rhonnie's grip and placed her hands on her sister's wet cheeks. Her watery eyes were red and Ahli knew hers probably looked the exact same.

"Sister, I need you right now, okay? We can't stay here."

"Okay," Rhonnie said, standing.

She turned away quickly so that she wouldn't have to see Quinton's body when she walked away. She willed herself to run up the stairs to the top level of the house. In the back of her mind she remembered hearing Brayland say that the house was clear; still, she was extra cautious with each step she took.

When she passed each room she observed that not only were the doors wide open and the lights on, but they were completely torn apart. From what it looked like from the doorways, however, nothing was taken. She continued her journey until she reached her father's bedroom, which, like the rest of the rooms, was completely ransacked. She sighed with relief when she saw that although some of the books had been knocked from the shelf most of them were still sitting upright. Particularly the one that she needed.

Shards of glass crunched under her feet with every step and with one look at the ground she saw that it was from the screen of the computer that had been smashed. Eventually she made it to the bookshelf and reached her hand for the smallest book on the shelf. It was an old children's rhyme book, so she understood why it had been left alone. Nobody would suspect that to be the lever to the secret room behind the shelf.

When she pulled it she heard the computer woman's voice speak through speakers on the sides of the shelf: "What is your favorite thing to do?"

Rhonnie cleared her voice and said, "Watch *Law & Order* with my daughters."

After a few moments she heard a clanking sound followed by a small hum before the bookshelf revealed itself as a secret doorway. Once it moved back she used her left hand to push it open the rest of the way. She wiped her face before she stepped foot into her father's war room. It was where they kept all of their weapons; he used to tell them that every thief should have a place like that. You never knew what kind of job you would have to do. The size of the room was about twelve feet by ten feet, and the lights shining down on her were brighter than she would have liked. In that room hanging from the walls there were automatic weapons all the way down to explosives.

In and out, she told herself. *In and out.*

She grabbed one of the army-print duffle bags hanging from the wall and started grabbing whatever she could fit in the bag: firearms, knives, and a boatload of ammunition. She didn't know who they would be up against, so a little bit of everything wouldn't hurt.

Once the bag was filled she took another bag off of the wall and loaded it with more ammunition for all of the firearms. Tossing the heavy bags over her shoulders she made to leave the room and head back downstairs, but a blinking light caught her attention. She glanced over and saw that her father's laptop was sitting under some papers. Something in Rhonnie couldn't leave it behind. She picked it up, along with its charger, and left, leaving the doorway open behind her.

Brayland and Ahli were waiting for her at the foot of the stairs when she finally bounded back down them. Ahli was holding a bag as well and when she saw Rhonnie staring she held it up and patted it.

"I grabbed all the pictures and other important stuff," she said. "I got Daddy's gun, too. It was in the basement. He must have left it there when he and Brayland were having drinks."

Rhonnie nodded, happy that her sister had thought to grab all of their memories, but sad to think that their father had died unarmed. He never stood a chance against whoever had done this.

"Here, let me take those," Brayland said. "Y'all got your car keys? Let's go."

"Where?" Rhonnie asked. "We don't have anywhere else to go."

"Yeah, we do," Ahli said, grabbing her sister by the hand. "Come on."

Chapter 9

"Daddy knew about your secret apartment?"

Rhonnie lay with her head resting peacefully on Ahli's stomach while Ahli stroked her hair. They both were still in the clothes that had Quinton's blood stained on them. For some reason neither wanted to take them off yet. Seeing the blood was a bittersweet reminder that their father had lived, but also that he was dead. All three of them had arrived at Ahli's apartment and had gathered in the guest bedroom. Rhonnie and Ahli occupied the bed while Brayland occupied a chair in the corner.

"No," Ahli answered her question.

"Yes," Brayland said from where he sat with his elbows on his knees and eyes on the floor. "He knew from the moment you signed your lease."

"What?" Ahli stopped her hand mid-stroke, genuinely surprised by this bit of information. She thought that the only reason Brayland found her that day was because he followed her.

"He knew the moment your credit report was pulled and when you signed your lease. He also knew when you went to the storage that he kept all of your mother's old things in."

"Why didn't he ever say anything?" Ahli was sure that Quinton would have figured it out eventually, yet she never would have guessed that he knew right out the gate.

"He wanted you to feel like you had something outside of all the chaos. He wanted you to feel like you had freedom."

Ahli smiled sadly to herself. She should have known that she wouldn't have been able to get anything like that by Quinton. Knowing him he probably had an extra key to her place, too.

"I feel so numb," Rhonnie whispered, looking at the ceiling. "I'm going to kill whoever did this to him."

"We have to find them first," Brayland's deep voice said.

"And when we do I'm going to cut their hearts out."

"Did Quinton have any enemies? And are you sure that nobody else knew where he lived?"

"Positive," Ahli responded. "And as far as enemies, no. Not that I know of, anyways. The only time his face has ever been out on a job was in Miami. When we made the exchange with Dot."

A look that Ahli couldn't read came over Brayland's face and he pulled his phone from his pocket. It was like he suddenly thought of something that he should have a long time ago. He shook his head in spite of himself and excused himself. "I'll be right back," he said and left the room.

"I can't believe we're alone," Rhonnie said. "He taught us everything except how to live without him."

"We aren't alone; we have each other."

Ahli leaned down and kissed Rhonnie's forehead. Even though the image of Quinton was embedded in her brain it just didn't seem real. He just couldn't be gone, not Quinton. Not everybody's hero. She didn't want Rhonnie to see her cry again, and that was exactly the reason why she had to leave the room before the tears were shed.

"Where are you going?" Rhonnie asked when Ahli was almost out of the room.

"I have to get out of these clothes," Ahli said over her shoulder. "I'm going to my room to take a shower. You can too if you want. The bathroom to this room is right there, and you can come to my room and get some clothes. Don't worry, you're safe."

"Okay." Rhonnie swallowed the lump in her throat. She didn't want to be left alone, but she understood that maybe her sister needed some time to herself. Or maybe she just wanted to be held by Brayland; either way, she wouldn't beg her to stay.

Once Ahli was gone Rhonnie shut the bedroom door to get some privacy. She lay back in the bed for a few more minutes with her eyes glued to the ceiling. Up until then she'd been trying to spare her own feelings, but she couldn't do that any longer. Her thoughts crept up on her as she reflected on one of the last conversations she had with her dad and the way she talked to him. If she had known that she wouldn't be able to wake up to him cooking breakfast the next day she would have treated him a little differently. Although they had made amends over the phone and she was able to say good-bye, it wasn't supposed to be for forever.

She clenched her eyes shut, trying to urge the sob not to come from her mouth, but that was almost impossible. She put one of the pillows over her face and held her stomach with one of her hands. She took one big breath and let it all out.

"Daddyyy," she sobbed into the pillow. "Not my daddy!"

She cried and rocked for about ten minutes until there was no more water available to leak from her eyes. She had so many emotions mixed up in her small body, but the rage was slowly but surely surfacing. Before it completely consumed her and she had the urge to do something stupid she figured that maybe taking Ahli's suggestion wouldn't be such a bad idea. Hopefully the hot water would wash away the images burned in her mind. Even better, maybe it would send her back in time.

She left the room and walked down the hallway to where her sister's bedroom was. She heard the shower running before she treaded onto the soft carpet of the room. In any other situation she would have smiled, as she had just noticed something. The bedrooms were fashioned just like their bedrooms were back at home. No wonder she felt so at home in the guest room. Because everything was the exact same. Rhonnie knew exactly where to find the articles of clothing she was looking for. Ahli, of course, had brand-new and never-worn under-wear in her drawer, along with bras and nightclothes.

She left as quietly as she came and headed back in the direction of her room. On the way she heard Brayland's voice coming from the living room but she didn't bother to stop and listen to his conversation. She closed her door again and went straight to the bathroom.

Rhonnie thought that a shower was what she needed, but almost as soon as she stepped in she wanted to get out and crawl back in bed. She hurried to finish her shower, scrubbing her skin until she felt raw all over, and then she got back out. She wrapped the purple towel around her body and kicked the bloodstained clothes behind the bathroom door and walked back into the room, drying her body off the whole way. Her wet hair dripped over her shoulders, but she didn't bother putting the towel to it. She just pulled the mock-jersey nightgown over her head after she put her underwear on.

The saddest part about the whole night was that she knew her father was still inside of the house staring aim-lessly into space. The room probably reeked by now and they would have to call someone in the morning to go get his body out of there. They didn't call the police because the manner of his murder was so sadistic that an entire investigation would have to happen. Right then they could use anything but the white man prodding his nose into their lives. If that happened it was a sure thing that they would never be able to get him out. Making a mental note to call his PO in the morning, she knew she would have to make up a lie about his death. Money talked so she was sure she'd be able to get it documented that he died however she wanted with what she had saved up.

"Who would do this to you, Daddy?" she asked the air around her.

She prepared to lie in bed and trace the ceiling until she reluctantly fell asleep, if she ever did. She drew the covers back to climb under them, but once again the blinking of the laptop caught her attention. Once they all had gotten into the apartment she'd placed it on the dresser that was against the far wall.

Before getting into the bed she grabbed the laptop, bringing it into the bed with her. Opening it up she knew that there would be a password to get into it, and after a few tries she was able to crack the code. The first thing that popped up was the background for his home screen. It was an old picture of the girls and their mother at the same park she was at earlier. That was what goaded her to click on his photo gallery and scroll through all of the pictures stored in the hard drive.

As she scrolled she told herself that she would get a USB drive and back up all the pictures to it. There were a lot of pictures that weren't framed in the bag that Ahli brought from the house; she couldn't risk losing them. When she clicked out of the gallery something told her to check on their bank accounts. She had that gut feeling again and she knew she should have just left well enough alone. When she saw the balances in the accounts she almost swallowed her tongue but instead she clenched her teeth and tried to swallow the misery.

"Fuck, man," she said, shaking her head. "Fuck!"

Just when she was about to close the laptop and throw it at a wall, her gaze fell on a folder labeled New Job. She clicked on it and realized that it contained the details from the last job Quinton was telling them about. She was staring smack dab at the blueprints all the way down to the digits for the safe that they were supposed to break into.

"He backed up the plans," Rhonnie said to herself, thinking back to the smashed-up computer in her dad's room.

Her father had always been a cautious and well-organized man. For that, she would always be thankful. She closed the laptop and leaped from the bed with it under her arm. Exiting the room she made her second trip down the hallway toward Ahli's room; that time she was going to make her presence known.

"LaLa!"

She was prepared to burst open the door, but she didn't have to since it was already open. Ahli was sitting up in her bed talking to Brayland. Once she heard Rhonnie's voice she turned her attention there with worry in her eyes.

"What, NaNa? Are you okay?" She got out of the bed and pushed past Brayland.

"I'm okay," Rhonnie told her. "What were you two talking about?"

"Brayland thought he knew who might have kil . . . done this to Daddy."

"Who?" Rhonnie's head whipped to Brayland. She was already mentally deciding which gun she would use to put a bullet in whoever's head it was. "Who did this?"

"I thought it was Dot," Brayland told them. "I was in the living room making some phone calls to a couple of niggas I trust back home. I was trying to see if Dot made any moves toward the Midwest."

"And?"

"It wasn't him."

"How do you know?"

"Because Dot is dead," he said. "They say his body was mailed to the front door of his house in a cardboard box."

Brayland's words took both of them by surprise. Brayland shrugged his shoulders in defeat and shook his head. "I guess somebody finally got to that nigga," he said in a faraway voice. "He had it coming if you ask me, but still even when I was calling around I knew it couldn't have been him."

Ahli resumed her position in her bed and Rhonnie scooted up the soft mattress until she was beside her. "How could you have known that if you didn't know he was dead? He was the last person that did bad business with my dad."

"I worked with Dot for a while," Brayland said, taking a seat at the computer desk to the left of the bed. "He was a cruel person, but the way Quinton was in that chair, he wouldn't do anything like that. He was the type of nigga who would put a bullet in your forehead and keep it pushing. I done seen a lot of dead bodies, and I can tell you that whoever did this to your old man wanted him to suffer. That comes from an emotional tie."

"Daddy didn't have a girlfriend," Ahli said. "He was always too busy."

"What about when you two were on jobs, you sure he wasn't messing with anybody?"

"Nah," Rhonnie said. "The only person he was getting pussy from was his PO. That's how he was able to come to Miami with us. He thought he was slick, but he wasn't."

"Would she want to hurt him?"

"No. She was married."

"Damn, I don't know then, y'all. Quinton was a good man. He ain't deserve to go out like this."

They sat in silence, lost in their own thoughts. Ahli took notice of the laptop in her bed and remembered that Rhonnie had something to say. "What did you want to talk about, NaNa?"

"Look," Rhonnie said, opening the laptop to show what she found.

"Daddy backed up all the plans for the next job in his laptop?" Ahli asked after viewing the file that Rhonnie showed her. "Why are you showing me this, Rhonnie?"

"Because of this," Rhonnie said and pulled up another screen, and then another, and then another.

When Ahli saw what she was being shown the gasp escaped her lips and she grabbed the laptop to get a closer look.

"Daddy had access to all of our main bank accounts on his main computer." Rhonnie crossed her legs and played with her thumbs. "Whoever murdered him wiped out all of our accounts. Transferred all of the money out. I have some money in another account, but not enough to live off of."

"What?" Ahli kept clicking back and forth between the screens. "No, this can't be possible. This can't be happening. All those jobs we went on. For nothing. Fuck!"

Ahli pushed the laptop forcefully from her and put her face in her palms. She wanted to cry, but she'd exhausted her ability to while she was in the shower. In her whole life she couldn't remember a time where she'd felt more defeated. She couldn't understand how someone could catch them slipping in such an unforeseen way. It just didn't make any sense.

She pulled her hands from her face and looked to her sister. She didn't know what to say and Rhonnie sighed, shrugging her shoulders.

"Daddy is dead and we're broke." Rhonnie looked from Ahli and then to Brayland. "I don't think we have a choice now."

"A choice about what?" Brayland asked.

"We have to do the job."

Chapter 10

"Okay, yes. Please lay new carpet down and just . . . just clean his body up nicely. Make him look as presentable as possible. My daddy didn't want a closed casket."

Rhonnie finished her phone conversation a few days later with the head of their cleaner team, Jacob. She'd worked with his team, of course, in the past but she was sure he was surprised when she called him and gave them the address to her own home the day after the massacre. He didn't ask many questions, but she heard the pain in his voice as they were discussing arrangements for Quinton's body. She was sure he heard the grief in hers too; making the arrangements for his body made it all real to her. Jacob told her that there was so much blood that it took two days to get it all up, but they made sure to get his body to the morgue first thing. Quinton was really gone, and soon his home would be a casket not fit for his greatness buried six feet underground.

Once everything was said and done, Rhonnie, Ahli, and Brayland all came to the same conclusion. Mentally they were all in sync with the fact that they were all out of options. They couldn't go back to the house simply because the sight of their father sitting dead in the living room, a place that they always came together to spend family time, was engraved in their skulls. It was a place where they once lived, but they could no longer call it home. Home was a place that provided comfort and security; that house had failed to do that. It would be going on the market as soon as they got back from Iowa.

The plan was simple: once they got to the hit they would get the money and get out. Ahli made contact with one of the guards of the house and let them know that the plan was still on. When asked what had caused the change of heart, she told them simply the love of money. Now heartless, Ahli knew that there was no way that the guards could live. They couldn't afford to split the money and, if they were just walking them in all willy-nilly, they couldn't be trusted anyways. The greed went both ways but she figured whoever's need for the money was greater, that would trump all.

"I'm sure once they see us they will make plans to pull the okie-doke on us too," Ahli said, reflecting on how Dot had done them. She leaned over the bar top in her kitchen, looking at Rhonnie, giving her a pep talk. "Especially when they see that Daddy isn't with us. But that's okay; we can just let them think that it will just be a walk in the park."

"Man, these people are always trying to get over on us!" Rhonnie said, tossing her phone to the side and picking up her father's pistol. It was the one she planned on using just in case things got out of hand. "Make us do all of the hard work and then pull the wool over our eyes."

"Yeah, well, that won't happen if I'm there," Brayland said, entering the kitchen carrying the duffle bags of guns and ammunition. "I'll put a bullet in anybody's head who even looks at you funny. I guess I gotta be the man of the house now."

The room suddenly grew quiet. He thought maybe he'd said the wrong thing and it was too soon to acknowledge the obvious. He, of course, had only known them all for such a short time but in that short time he'd grown closer to them than he'd been with anybody in his life. He used to only put in work because he knew he was getting paid for it; now he was doing it because he wanted to. The least he could do for Quinton was continue to make sure his daughters were safe, which he didn't mind doing at all. After all, they had taken him in like a stray and made sure he was fed, housed, and clothed. They didn't have to do that. There were people he'd known for years who never cared about his well-being, people who would have left him in that parking lot to die. They didn't have to invite them to their dinner table, and Quinton didn't have to put him in a fly whip. But he did and as a rule of trade he wouldn't be going anywhere until God made him. The feeling that Ahli gave him was one that he didn't want to go away from anytime soon, and he felt the need to protect Rhonnie like a kid sister. He stood where he was staring at the two of them making preparations and he accepted the fact that they were the only people in his corner.

"Good," Rhonnie finally responded, giving Brayland an approving nod. "I'm sure my dad wouldn't have wanted it any other way. I'll be right back."

She jumped down from the barstool she was sitting on and brushed past him and headed toward the direction of the bedrooms. Brayland waited for her to leave to go around the bar and wrap his muscular arms around Ahli's waist from behind. Something he noticed about her when he first met her was that she rarely showed any sign of weakness when Rhonnie was around. He brought it up awhile back and she told him simply, "She needs me to be strong. I can't let her see me weak. I'm her rock."

It dawned on him that she was always so busy trying to be strong for everyone around her that she didn't realize she needed her own rock to lean on. That was something that made him want to stay around even more. He had already explored the depths of her ocean; now times were giving him a reason to intertwine with her soul.

She allowed him to hug her. At first he felt her tense up, but slowly he felt her relax in his arms. He'd held her all night just like that as well, with his face nestled in her warm neck, and for a few hours time seemed to stand still. When the morning came and she woke up in a fit of screams, he was there to soothe her and wipe away her tears. She was still the same woman he'd met that day on Dot's block; her heart was just broken.

"You sure you can handle this?" he asked, kissing the nape of her neck.

"Yes," Ahli responded, closing her eyes. She placed her hands on top of his. "I mean, I have to. Especially since we still don't know who murdered my father. It will be good to leave the city for a few days. For all we know we could be sitting ducks right now. You know you don't have to come, right?"

"I do have to."

"No, you don't. Rhonnie and I can handle ourselves."

"I never said you couldn't, but anything could happen. And if something were to happen to you I'd . . ."

He paused and Ahli opened her eyes. She turned around in his arms to face him, connecting her gaze with his. She placed her soft hands on his cotton shirt over his chest and leaned into him. There was something about the intense way that he stared down at her that gave her goose bumps, and not the bad kind. The kind that made her never want him to let her go. The kind that made her want to cling to him forever. "You'd what?"

Brayland leaned down and put his forehead gently on hers, inhaling the vanilla scent coming from her melanin. His eyes focused on her lips, not able to look in her eyes any longer. He never thought a woman could have him open the way that she did; it was an affection he'd never felt toward anyone. He left one hand on the small of her back and brought the other to her face, using his thumb to massage her cheek tenderly.

"I'd go crazy." His tone was serious and his jaw clenched. "I don't know. Ever since I met you shit in my life has changed. When I was back in Miami I used to wake up with one purpose: get money. That was it. I was only living to make a dollar, and that's no way to live. Because what if I woke up broke one day? There would be no happiness in my life."

"And now?" Ahli's breathing was in sync with his. "What gives you purpose?"

"Now I live to see that smile on your face. Shit, I wanna be the nigga to put it there. I was never one to believe in fate until that day you drove into the hood in that gold Camaro. You were mine then and you're mine now. Understand? So yes, I have to go with you."

"Bray—"

He shut her up swiftly by pulling her face up to his, forcing her on the tips of her toes. Her lips felt so soft on his and they were the sweetest things he'd ever tasted. He pulled back from her and saw that her doe-shaped eyes were still shut, almost as if his kiss had left her in a trance.

"I'm yours too," he breathed down at her. "I will follow you to the fuckin' moon and back. Guns blazing, nigga. I'm a grown man. I can make my own decisions. Today and every day after, I choose you. You're the best thing I never knew I needed."

"I only gave it to you one time." Ahli finally opened her eyes. "You're whipped already?"

Brayland was caught off guard by her response. He was even more shocked when he saw the smile spread on her face, simply because it was something he hadn't seen in days. Her eyes were still mournful, but he knew it would take some time for that to go away. Still, he would take it as it came and he grinned back at her.

"I guess you can say that," he said, kissing her again. "That shit is golden, ma."

The two of them embraced and didn't break apart until Rhonnie came back and resumed her seat at the bar. She placed the laptop on the bar top in front of her as she scrolled through the folder with the plans.

"We need to be there by tomorrow at three," Rhonnie told them. "That's when our guy's shift starts. The drive is a few hours so I say we leave late tonight so we're already there. We can set up and be ready before then."

Ahli came around the bar so that she too could look at the plans. She would question why Rhonnie wanted to leave so soon if the hit wasn't until the afternoon the next day, but secretly she knew why. She didn't want to be in that city longer than she had to. It had caused them so much pain over the last few days, a change of scenery was much needed.

"Okay," she said, looking across the kitchen at the digital clock over the stove. It read thirty minutes until six. "We need to finish getting ready then. I'm thinking one car should be cool."

Rhonnie clicked out of the file and their eyes were glued on the screensaver. She felt the lump forming in the back of her throat again. She gripped the edge of the bar and breathed deeply.

"They ripped his throat out." She finally said it out loud. "They ripped his fucking throat out. Who would do some sick shit like that?"

"I don't know." Ahli tried not to think about her father's gaping neck. "And that's why we gotta go get this money, so we can move around. It was just by chance that we weren't at the house when they came for Daddy. After we get back I say we bury Daddy, sell the house, and move on from here."

"Not until I find out who killed him."

"You'll be chasing a ghost. The security footage had already been wiped clean."

"Exactly! So we might be on their list too!"

"No." Ahli shook her head. "Nobody except Uncle Lance even knew Daddy had daughters. Did you ever notice that both of their names were always spelled wrong on our information when we were in school?"

"Yeah, because the schools never updated their systems."

"Or maybe our parents purposely kept us secret," Ahli said, thinking about the story Quinton told her. "Maybe they were trying to protect our identities. I think whoever killed him was just after him. And they got him. It will be hard, but he taught us how to survive for a reason. The only thing we can do is move on."

"Where?"

"I don't know, but with half a million dollars we can go anywhere."

Chapter 11

Two Days Earlier

A man sat behind his desk filing some paperwork that he'd been putting off for weeks when he heard the door to his office open.

"Honey, I'm working," he said, not looking up. "I said I'll be down in a little bit."

"No need." An ominous voice he didn't recognize filled the air. "I like you right where you are."

His head jerked up in time to see what was probably the most beautiful woman he'd ever seen in his life. She wore a gray skirt suit with a ruffled white collared shirt and she had her clutch purse tucked under her armpit. The tall white and gray stiletto pumps made her look much taller than she was and the suit showed off the kind of curves that would drive any man insane. Her mahogany brown skin was smooth and her high cheekbones made her full red lips pop without question. She had jet-black hair pulled into a tight bun with two sticks protruding from it. Her appearance made it hard to determine her age but her slanted, cold brown eyes belonged to a person who had seen much death.

"And you are?"

"It does not matter who I am, Lance," the woman said, walking to the desk and wiping the papers from it in one swipe so that she could sit down. "All that matters right now is who you are."

The smile she gave him was an eerie one and he was certain he'd never seen this woman a day in his life. He didn't know who she was or how she even knew his name. "How do you know my name?"

"Ohhh." She chuckled, leaning back on one of her hands. "A little birdie might have let it slip."

"Bitch, I'm not going to play your little games." Lance reached for the landline phone next to his desktop computer so that he could call security to have her escorted out. "You need to get the hell out of my office."

"I wouldn't do that if I were you," she told him and admired her favorite red polish on her nails.

As soon as he put the phone to his ear, he expected to hear the dial tone. When he heard nothing, he pressed some of the buttons on the base of the phone; but still there was nothing but dead air. At first, when he saw the woman enter, he wasn't intimidated at all. Now all he wanted to know was who in the world she was and how she was able to get past his security. Two big men sat at the gate that surrounded his entire property and two more stood in front of the door, making sure that nobody who was uninvited made it through.

He looked at the woman sitting on his desk casually looking at her small hands and then at his computer screen. Clicking a few buttons he brought up the camera views from the front of the house and by the gate. What he saw made his stomach turn. All four men were in plain view, except they were lying in awkward angles on the ground by their posts. He could see that their throats had been slit and that they were lying in thick pools of their own blood.

"Tsk, tsk, tsk." The woman shook her head at him. "And I hoped you would make this easy for me."

"Who the fuck are you? And what do you want?" Lance growled. The jaw line on his chocolate face clenched and beads of sweat were forming on top of his bald head.

The woman noticed his perspiration and smirked. "No need to be nervous. As long as you do everything I say you won't have anything to worry about. Now"—she stood and walked around the desk until she was standing directly in front of him—"the birdie who sang that beautiful song in my ear told me that you know a man by the name of Quinton Malone."

Never in his life had he felt fear because of a woman, but there was something about the one in front of him that made his skin crawl. She stared down her pointy nose at him and something in him said that she would do whatever she needed to do to get the information she wanted. His dead men proved that. Still, he and Quinton went way back. It would take more than a few sliced necks for him to give his friend up. "I've never heard that name in my life."

"Ohhh, a thief and a liar." She wrinkled her nose. "So naughty, but I guess those traits do go hand in hand. Now I'm going to ask you a different question, and this time keep in mind that I know what kind of business you do together."

"Fuck you," he spat. "You killed my men. I'm not telling you anything."

"You don't need to tell me anything, but you will tell him something."

At that point she untucked her clutch from under her arm so that she could retrieve a folded-up piece of paper from it. When she dropped it in his lap she motioned for him to open it up. After glaring at her for a few more moments, curiosity got the best of him and he did as she wanted. Scrawled in black ink with neat black handwriting were details to a job in Coralville, Iowa. It stated that there was a vault of some kind with half a million dollars in it.

"Is this real?" he asked, greed getting the best of him.

"Nope." She sat down on his lap and looked deeply into his eyes. "But you're going to make it sound like it."

Her hand trailed down his face, to his chest, and stopped for a second at his crotch. She let out a small laugh when she felt that his little member was standing directly up and at full attention. It always amused her how easy it was to arouse a man, even in a seemingly life-or-death situation. She wondered if it was her plump bottom or her perky breasts that was making him horny. She knew that even though he'd seen with his own two eyes that his guards were dead, the only reason why he hadn't thrown her from his lap was because he wanted her sexually. He had sexualized her from the moment she stepped foot in his office, even though his family was currently under the same roof. She looked in his eyes as she stroked his manhood, making him swallow hard before she moved her hand to its real destination. Pulling his cell phone from his pocket, she shoved it into his chest.

"Call him now," she demanded without question.

"And if I don't?" he asked.

She smiled at him and cocked her head. "Did I mention that it wasn't me who killed your guards?"

"If you didn't, then who did?"

The woman leaned away from him slightly to click a button on his keyboard. She clicked through a few screens, casually passing the ones with the views of his cooks and housekeepers also lying dead in their own blood. She zoomed in on one of the views from the cameras in the house and revealed a sight even more horrible than the first. Huddled in the living room on the couch were his wife and daughter, which would have been a normal sight, except they were not alone.

Standing over them was a masked woman holding a bloody machete. On her waist it was apparent that she had a firearm as well. The woman stood up from him so that she could get a good look at his face. She was pleased at the horror displayed there. She tried to capture the moment of his eyes widening so that she could hold on to it forever.

"Now make the call."

Lance finally peeled his eyes from the screen and looked back at the woman. He weighed his options. Not only had he been in situations like the one at hand, but he was usually the one doing the demanding. With that being said he knew there was a slim chance to none that any of them would make it out of there alive. He took a breath and spit at her feet.

"Go fuck ya'self, bitch," he told her, putting his hand on the dcsk, fixing to stand up.

She was growing tired of his inability to cooperate, because she was not used to such disobedience. She was Madame. What she said went, and nobody said no to her. The rage filled her heart so suddenly and Lance didn't have time to move his hand away. She pulled one of the instruments from her hair, revealing that it was really a long, sharp knife, and she brought it down with all her might.

"Awwh!" he screamed in agony when she impaled his hand against the desk.

Tears immediately came to his eyes as the pain set in and he tried to pull the knife from his hand. All that did was make the pain even more excruciating. He sat there trying not to move, panting with gritted teeth.

"I did not say that you could get up," she snarled and pushed him back into his seat. "This is a nice office you have here. I would hate to repaint it in your blood."

She pulled out her own phone from her clutch, pressed a button, and put the receiver to her ear. From where he sat he could see the woman with the machete answer the phone.

"Bring them up here," the woman instructed and disconnected the call.

Minutes later his wife and daughter were being pushed on the floor of his office. Both had tears streaming from their faces, and they were shaking in fear.

"Lance, what's going on! What have you done?" his wife, Tanya, screamed at him. "Who are these people and what are they doing in our home?"

"Daddy!" his daughter, Tiffany, screamed from where she lay on the floor. She saw his hand and the blood oozing from it and her eyes expelled panic. "Daddy, they killed all the workers. I saw Olivia on the ground when they brought us up here. Please do whatever they say. I don't want to die!"

Lance's brow furrowed and he tried to eat the pain shooting up his left arm. He felt like a horrible parent. It seemed that his life of doing bad deeds had finally caught up to him. He looked at his nineteen-year-old daughter's face and knew that, unlike him, she deserved to live a long life. He wished that he'd let her go off to stay in the college dorms over summer break. Now there was no telling if any of them would get out of this situation.

"Listen to your daughter," the woman in the dress suit told him.

"Goddammit, Lance, do what she tells you!" his wife shrieked when he once again hesitated.

"Okay," he finally said. "Okay. I'll call him."

"Good," the woman said and, once again without warning, snatched the blade from his hand.

"Fuck!" he howled. "Fuck!"

The woman was unmoved by his grimaces; however, she allowed him a few moments to get himself together. Once his breathing was in order he looked again to his family on the ground and then to the phone in his lap. Knowing he had no other choice, he picked up the phone to dial the number to Quinton's cell phone.

"Before you make that phone call I must ask one question," the woman interrupted him just as he was about to dial the number. "Is it true that the girl Dot shot was his daughter?"

"Yes," Lance answered, not seeing a point in lying.

"And is Rhebecca truly dead?"

"Yes."

The woman nodded and signaled for him to continue making the call. Once Quinton answered she was prepared to stick the blade in Lance's neck if he tried any funny business. However, she was pleased by his performance.

"Nothing much, man," Lance responded in a rushed tone. "Just tryin'a see how you're living. I heard about what happened down in Miami. Bruh, I swear on my mother that if I knew that nigga was on foul play like that I would have never sent you."

She listened to him read off the details from the piece of paper and, by the time he was finished, she wished she could give him an Oscar. When he hung up the phone he looked up to the woman with hot tears coming from his eyes.

"I just betrayed one of my best friends," he said, scrunching his face up. "Why are you doing this?"

"Because long ago your best friend stole something from me," she told him, snatching the phone from his hand before strutting around the desk and toward the door. "And I want it back."

Lance noticed that she was exiting the room by herself and that the woman with the machete was advancing on him. "Wait, you said you wouldn't hurt us! We had a deal!"

The woman stopped in the doorway and turned her head so that she could look back over her shoulder. "I said I wouldn't hurt you. I didn't say anything about her."

She turned to the woman dressed in black from head to toe, except for the white mask on her face. "Make it messy, Tamia. You have two minutes."

She gave a sinister laugh and allowed her stilettos to stab the carpet under her feet as she walked away from the massacre waiting to happen. She barely heard the first gunshot or the screams that followed coming from behind her. She was too busy thinking about the way her plan was about to unfold.

Chapter 12

Ahli glanced in the rearview mirror and was given the image of her sister asleep in the back seat of the BMW. Her head was leaned against the window and Ahli imagined that it was cold on her forehead. Rhonnie's expression was peaceful, the most peaceful she'd seen it in days, and that granted her solitude.

Averting her eyes back to the highway ahead of her she focused on the path the bright lights were leading her to. The GPS in the vehicle said they were a little over an hour away, giving them an arrival time of midnight. She sighed and tried to listen to the music playing softly from the speakers, but she couldn't focus on any of the lyrics because of the loud pitter-patter of the rain hitting the car. She began to think about how her life had changed so drastically in the course of three days.

Her future was looking more and more like the road she was driving on; she didn't know what was around the bend. Whenever she tried to think about what would happen after this last job she came up blank. She was ready to live a normal life, like Rhonnie always talked about, but exactly what was a normal life? Would she still be able to sleep soundly like a baby? Or would she have nightmares for the rest of her life? The identity she currently had was who she'd been for so long that she didn't know how to be anybody else. What happened to her father should have been an eye-opener and instilled fear in her heart. Instead, she harbored rage. A rage that needed an outlet; so would she ever be normal?

"You know you'll be all right, don't you?"

Brayland's groggy voice interrupted her thought process. He had dozed off for a while, but he'd been up for a few minutes just watching her facial expressions change. He couldn't begin to imagine the thoughts in her head, but he had a good idea that none of them were good.

"How can you be so sure?"

"Because I know when things like this happen the worst place you can go is backward. There isn't a point in chasing the past," he told her, thinking about his own life.

"But I'm so mad," Ahli breathed, scrunching up her face and trying to keep her tears in check. She didn't remember a time when she cried so much. "I should have been there. I should have saved him!"

"You can't blame yourself for this, Ahli." Brayland's voice was stern. "You said it yourself: Quinton was a man who did many things, things that some wouldn't be too proud of. Stop beating yourself up, because when it comes down to it you can't change the fact that he's dead. Love him, mourn him, and remember him for the man he was. But don't ever get caught up in telling yourself what could have happened. You'll drive yourself crazy."

"You don't know what you're talking about. You don't know the half of what I'm feeling so don't try to fucking tell me how I should handle anything!"

"I don't?" The vein in Brayland's temple showed and he breathed deeply, turning his head to look out the window. He knew everything was still so fresh in her mind and she might have just needed an outlet for her anger but, still, what she said definitely struck a nerve for him. He focused on the trees slightly blowing in the night breeze as she pushed eighty on the highway, and he thought about just letting what she said go.

Fuck that, he thought, and turned his head back to her. "Maybe I don't know what you're going through or how you're feeling, but let me switch shit up for you right quick. In the line of work that you do, how many men have you killed? How many funerals have you been the cause of? How many fathers do you think you took from some little girl? Now you know how they feel."

Ahli's breath got caught in her airway. She wanted, needed, to say something, but she couldn't find the words. Her hand twitched on the steering wheel because she had the sudden urge to slap him for speaking to her in such a way. But she couldn't. She couldn't because he was right and that was the toughest pill to swallow.

"It's an unruly exchange, but sometimes we cash in on the horrible things we've done in the worst ways. Quinton's death being one of them."

"So you're telling me to just get over the fact that I saw my father stabbed to death in his favorite chair a few days ago?"

"No. What I'm saying is that unless you have a time machine there is nothing you can do to change the fact that it happened. No matter how much you cry or take your anger out on others it, ain't never gon' change that fact."

"So what am I supposed to do? Just forget."

"Nah. You're going to get this money. And I'm going to help."

Ahli nodded but didn't say a word at first, for fear that her voice would betray her. She didn't speak again until she was sure she had control of her emotions. "After the job is over, are you going to leave?"

"Not even if you asked me to," he replied, placing a hand on her thigh and squeezing it affectionately.

She turned her eyes from the road for two seconds so that she could smile and nod at him. "Okay. After th—"

Boom!

The sound of the tires blowing drowned out what she was trying to say and she temporarily lost control of the car. They began to swerve violently and she gripped the steering wheel, trying to keep them all from going off of the road and into a ditch. She veered too far left and drove the vehicle straight into the headlights of an oncoming semi truck.

In the back seat, Rhonnie had woken up and screamed when she saw the truck headed straight for them. Ahli used her whole body to turn the steering wheel all the way right, swerving the car before they hit the semi head-on. When she was able to finally pull over on the side of the road she cut the engine off and let her forehead fall to the top of the steering wheel, breathing heavily. Her heart felt as though it were going 500 miles per hour in her chest, and she couldn't get the sick feeling out of the pit of her stomach. From behind her she felt Rhonnie's hands on her shoulders, pulling her back so that she was sitting straight up in her seat.

"Wh . . . what the hell was that?" Rhonnie breathed into Ahli's hair when she wrapped her arms around her sister and hugged her tight. "What just happened?" Ahli didn't answer her but Rhonnie could feel her heart throbbing under her wrists. It made her hug her big sister even tighter.

"You got a flashlight in here, Rhonnie?" Brayland asked, looking around.

"Yeah, right there in the glove compartment."

"A'ight," he said when he had the long black flashlight in his hands. "Y'all stay here."

Brayland opened his door and got out to check out the damage on the vehicle. The girls saw the light from the flashlight moving around in front of the vehicle for a few seconds and prayed silently for the best.

Rhonnie let go of Ahli and leaned back in her seat. Her heart was beating fast and she was grateful for the miss. Not for herself—she was ready for the pain within her heart to be ended—but she was grateful that nothing happened to Ahli. Rhonnie sighed and watched the flashlight moving around the car, and it reminded her of police officer's bright light looking for any reason to book them. She just hoped the damage to the car wouldn't be too bad. When Brayland returned, completely drenched from the rain, to the car, the look on his face didn't offer them any reassurance.

"How bad?" Ahli asked.

Brayland shook his head. "Bad. Looks like you hit something sharp in the road. Both tires are done for and the bottom of grill is fucked up from skidding on the concrete like that."

"I have insurance," Rhonnie chimed in. "I can call my provider and get someone sent out to us."

"Nobody is gon' come in a storm like this for some hours," he said. "And I don't know about you, but I'm not waiting here for that long without food and shit."

"Okay, well, where are we gon' go then, Sherlock? We're in the middle of nowhere!"

Ahli could hear them going back and forth but she wasn't really paying attention. All she could think of was that it was her fault that the car was messed up. If only she hadn't taken her eyes off of the road, she would have been able to divert from whatever she'd run over in the road.

"Dammit!" She banged on the steering wheel with her fists, causing the whole car to shake. "Shit!"

Brayland grabbed a hold of her arms and held them although she tried to break free. "Hey." Brayland gripped her wrists tight. "Hey! Stop!"

"Yeah, stop it, Ahli! It will be okay!"

"No! No, it won't be! I just fucked everything up!"

"No, you didn't," Rhonnie said, pointing to the clock in the car. "It's only ten o'clock. If I call them now they'll for sure be here by the morning and we can hit the road again. We will be okay, sister. We're going to make this job even if it kills us."

"Or not." Brayland looked at Rhonnie like she was crazy before pulling Ahli to his chest and stroking the back of her head. "We're gon' be all right. First thing we need to do is get out of this car before a state patrol officer finds us."

"Yeah, imagine trying to explain why we have all of these unlicensed weapons in here. I think I have some umbrellas in my trunk, and maybe even some rain ponchos."

Ahli nodded in Brayland's shoulder and pulled away from him. She knew they were both right. They needed to leave.

"I think I saw something back there that said there might be some restaurants and motels up farther that way. That will be our best bet until someone can make it out to help us with the tires."

"Okay. I'll make the call now."

While Rhonnie was in the car on the phone with her insurance company, Ahli and Brayland were rummaging around in the trunk for the umbrellas and ponchos. The thunder and lightning accented their moods and the rain was coming down so hard that it was difficult to hear anything around them.

"Here!" Brayland yelled when he finally found the army-print ponchos. "Put this on!"

There weren't any umbrellas but the ponchos had hoods on them, and that would have to be good enough. He handed her the lighter of the two duffle bags and threw the heavy one on his own shoulder. The only thing on his mind was getting out of the rain. He waited for Ahli to give the other poncho to Rhonnie so they could start their hike to nobody knew where.

"You were right!" Rhonnie yelled over the rain. "They said they can't send anyone out until the storm is over! And that most likely won't be until the morning!"

They began to walk in a single-file line, much like the way most kids do in elementary school, being sure not to get too far away from each other. At first Brayland wanted to clown Rhonnie for the kind of ponchos she had in her trunk; however, they helped when it came to the heavy rain that was falling around them.

They walked for at least fifteen minutes without coming up on any buildings, and Ahli kept trying to reassure herself that they just needed to go a little farther. There had to be a gas station or something they would be able to stop at. When the twenty-five-minute mark was coming up she was about ready to head back to the car. She turned around with a completely wet face to tell them that she thought that maybe she was mistaken, but she was blinded by a pair of headlights slowing to a stop next to them. They all took a step back, not knowing who was on the other side of the window, but when it rolled slowly down they became at ease.

"What are you guys doing out in a storm like this?" a young woman called out. It was dark, but her golden brown skin seemed to pop in the flashing lightning. She had luscious, full lips, pretty brown eyes, and her straight hair was pulled back into a neat ponytail.

"Our car broke down back there!" Brayland replied.

"That BMW? I just drove past it not too long ago! Where are you guys headed?"

"Just to find shelter until we can start moving again in the morning!"

"I know a place!" she yelled. "You guys were headed in the right direction because it's actually not too far from here! I can give you a lift if you want."

Brayland looked at the girls to see if it was okay with them.

"Boy, if you don't get in the damn car!" Rhonnie pushed past him and got in the front seat of the Toyota. "Come on! I'm not trying to be in this rain for another second!"

"Here, let me pop the trunk. You can stuff your bags back there!"

Once they were all safely in the dry car, the woman pulled off in the same direction that they were going.

"Thank you so much. We really appreciate it!" Rhonnie said, studying the woman's profile.

"No worries," she replied. "I'm just glad I was around to help. What happened to your car, anyways?"

"My sister ran over something in the street," Rhonnie said, shaking her head. "Blew out both of the tires and almost got us killed by a semi truck."

"Well, now." The woman laughed. "Forgive me for laughing but that sounds like an eventful night."

"Yeah, tell us about it," Ahli said from the back seat.

They drove for about five more minutes until they finally reached the apparent destination. Although Ahli was wary at first to get into the car with a complete stranger, she realized they would have been walking for at least twenty more minutes and that would have been horrible.

"We're here," the woman said in a cheery voice. She pulled around the circular bend and parked her car in front of the tall double doors.

"Whoa," Rhonnie said when she saw it. It was the most elegant building she'd ever seen in her life. It looked like something out of a movie and it reminded her of a place that should have been in Paris, or Italy. Not in the middle of nowhere in a place like Iowa. The brick on the building was painted a rose gold and in the middle of the top of it were glass windows shaped in a dome.

"Such a beautiful place, huh? I thought so too my first time here," the woman said, her voice distant.

Rhonnie took her eyes away from the building just in time to see the sadness in the woman's eyes. But it was only there for a brief second and Rhonnie questioned if she even saw it there. The woman popped the trunk and unlocked all of their doors so that they could get out.

"Thank you so much," Ahli said from outside of the car. "I feel so rude; you picked us up and helped us and we didn't even get your name."

The woman looked at each one of them standing outside of the tall doors, letting her eyes linger on Brayland before putting her eyes back on Ahli. "My name is Anna," she told her before putting her car back into drive and pulling away. "Welcome to the Opulent Inn."

Chapter 13

She watched through one of the security cameras in her room as they walked into the inn, wet and tired. Very much like their father had done all those years ago. She tapped her long, freshly painted red nails together and squinted her eyes at the screen.

"It's crazy how fate has a way of playing out, isn't it?"

"Yes, Madame," one of her oldest girls, Tamia, said from where she sat on a stool.

She was sitting on a stool while Madame sat on her oversized bed. Tamia was trying her best to paint Madame's toe nails to perfection, like she had done with her fingernails. Knowing that if she messed up in the tiniest way Madame would strike her for the mistake, she finished the final toe in excellence.

"This is truly such a beautiful color on you, Madame," Tamia said, setting Madame's foot down softly. She smiled down at the great job she had just done and hoped that Madame would be pleased as well. She should have known better, though. Madame was never pleased.

"Shut up, Tamia," Madame said absentmindedly, still staring at one of the flat TV screens on her wall. "A five-year-old could paint my toes, with still hands at that."

"I . . . I am sorry I have displeased you, Madame." Tamia swallowed, thinking of how to get back in Madame's good graces. "Would you like to take a warm bath?"

"Do you see those women?" she asked, completely ignoring Tamia's statement. When Tamia nodded, she continued, "After you put the top coat on I want you to go down and welcome them as our new guests. I will have one of the other girls get their accommodations ready."

"What girls will you be assigning to them, Madame?"

"Oh, they won't be needing our special services." Madame chuckled to herself. "Well, actually, maybe he does. But the other two? They are here to repay an old debt to me."

"What kind of debt, Madame?"

Madame eyed the top of Tamia's head and wondered when she had become so nosey. Ever since she'd become Madame's closest pet all those years ago she seemed to have forgotten who and what Madame was.

Once Tamia was done applying the top coat she looked up at Madame, wondering why she had stopped talking. When she did she was met with a backhand to the face that was so powerful she was knocked off of the stool. Her shaking hand flew to her stinging face, and she tried to crawl backward when Madame stood. Tamia's eyes looked around the room for a weapon that Madame might use to punish her with so that she could prepare herself for the type of pain to come.

"Don't ever ask me questions," Madame said sinisterly, standing over her. "Or the other girls will be asking each other how you died."

Tamia held her breath and blinked repeatedly, trying to hold Madame's cold gaze. She knew there was no way to win in that situation; the only thing she could do was lie there like a sitting duck. She tensed herself, but Madame didn't strike her again. Instead, she sat back down on her bed and watched as one of the girls repeatedly pressed on the bell in hopes of getting a worker's attention.

Madame watched too in silence. After leaving Lance's house she was pleased with herself, but that feeling was short-lived. She'd taken Lance's phone to communicate to Quinton like she was Lance to make sure he traveled the path that she needed him to. Imagine her surprise when she received the message from him saying that he was no longer interested in doing the job and that maybe he should give someone else a chance to get all that money. The anger she felt right then was unmatched, and she knew there was only one thing left to do. She was too far away to handle it, but she knew one person who wasn't.

She found Quinton's address through files in Lance's home and sent Anna on the two-hour drive to do her bidding. She was to torture them all until she was given the location of what Madame needed. The night Rhebecca ran away she stole $50,000 from her safe, but that wasn't what Madame was worried about. She didn't care about what was taken from her safe; she was more concerned about what Rhebecca failed to leave there.

For years Madame searched for it and a part of her regretted having her kill the man who had come up with the perfect drug. A drug that would allow her to spread her influence to everyone she came into contact with. The drug that would ultimately put her in control of all men. Every dirty, filthy, sex-driven man in the world would be hers. They would fear her, but most importantly they would respect her without paying attention to what she had between her legs.

"Call up to the girls' quarters. I want someone to greet them. It's going to get . . . loud tonight. And not in the usual way, so have Anna get rid of the few guests we have."

"But, Madame, there is a storm outside. Where will they go?"

"I never said make them leave." Madame gave Tamia a menacing look, letting her know exactly what she meant. She glanced down at the diamond-studded watch on her wrist. She watched Tamia as she stood back up. The pink lace lingerie she wore fit a little snug as Tamia had grown thicker over the years. Still it looked good on her, good enough to eat. "Tell Anna to make sure she gets the money first before she disposes of them. I'll have about thirty minutes to spare while all of this is going on. Once the calls are made, come back to me."

It didn't take long to distribute Madame's orders. Anna had just returned to her room when Tamia called upon her saying that her services were needed once again.

"All done, Madame." Tamia turned to face Madame.

She saw that Madame too was now dressed in nothing but her underwear and bra. Although in her early forties, Madame's body put all of her girls' bodies to shame. Her breasts were full and sat up perfectly, her stomach was flat, and she was shaped like a Coca-Cola bottle, making any man whose eyes graced her body thirsty. There was only one blemish on her whole body: a healed-up cut on her neck. A wound she obtained a long time ago, one that reminded her every day that no man could be forgiven.

"I want your face," Madame told her. "Show me how you please the men who come to see you."

She waved Tamia to her with her pointer finger and Tamia happily obliged. Madame only let her favorite girls please her and Tamia was just happy to once again be in her good graces. "Anything for you, Madame."

When the two women were standing directly in front of each other, Madame placed the same finger under Tamia's chin and gently lifted her head up. "You know I hate hurting you girls, right?" Madame asked her, letting her hands travel down Tamia's voluptuous body. "I just hate when you are disobedient to me. I am the only one who has ever cared about you. I am the only one who has ever loved you. Everything I do is to give you girls power. As long as you have power you will have respect. Understand? After tonight we will have that."

"Yes, Madame." Tamia closed her eyes and relished the feeling of Madame's soft hands fondling her body. "I understand."

"I know you do," Madame whispered and unhooked Tamia's bra.

When her breasts were released Madame could feel herself growing moist between her legs, something no man had been able to do since the incident. She let her hands massage and pinch away at Tamia's nipples as she watched her face twist up in a satisfied grimace. Tamia's eyes were shut and her breath quickened when she felt Madame's lips wrap around her erect nipple.

"Oh, Madame," she moaned, feeling Madame's tongue going in circular motions on each one of her breasts. "Please don't stop."

The sound of Madame's slurping filled the air and she placed her hand gently between Tamia's legs, rubbing her there tenderly. It was moist and warm down there, just as she had expected. She blocked out Tamia's moans of pleasure and focused on her own bliss. She pulled Tamia's pink panties to the side and used her middle finger to tickle her wet clit while she still sucked her breasts. By pleasing Tamia she was turning herself on even more. She was in total control, and she was loving every minute of it. It was amazing how the sexual organs were equivalent to game controllers. By being in command of somebody sexually meant you could make them do whatever you wanted them to. By dominating their mind they would lie for you, steal for you, kill for you.

Tamia's moans snapped Madame back into the moment. She had just tossed her head back when suddenly Madame gripped her by the hips and tossed her on the bed behind her.

"Put your face in the pillows and bend over," Madame whispered.

When Tamia did as she was instructed Madame went to her nightstand and grabbed what she needed from it. Once she removed her panties and the strap was securely around her waist, she climbed on the bed and approached the round brownness smiling at her. She gripped both of Tamia's cheeks and spread them open before bending over herself and putting her face in it. She licked and slurped at Tamia's beautiful kitten until she shook violently.

"Ahhh! Madame!" Tamia squealed into the pillow and tried to writhe her body away, but Madame's grip was too strong. "I'm coming! I'm comingggg!"

Madame sucked at her clit one more time before sitting back up straight on her knees and inserting the strap in from behind. She long stroked Tamia better than any man ever had and made her claw at the headboard. Every thrust caused Tamia to arch her back even more until her chest was begging the bed for refuge. The suction of the strap-on was kissing Madame's clit, bringing her closer and closer to her own climax until finally she couldn't hold it anymore. She pulled out of Tamia and snatched the strap off. Tamia already knew what to do when she heard it hit the ground and saw Madame lie on the bed. Even with shaky legs she whipped around on all fours and put her mouth on Madame's throbbing love button.

Madame gripped the back of her head and squirted all of her sweet juices on Tamia's face and in her mouth. She bit her lip and clenched her eyes shut to hold in her moans, but that only made her body quiver even harder.

"Mmm, Madame," Tamia whispered, planting kisses on Madame's exposed pussy. "You taste like heaven."

Madame let her lick a few more times before pushing her away. She stood up from the bed almost as if nothing had just taken place and looked down at Tamia's naked body blankly.

"Get dressed and make sure everything is in place."

"Yes, Madame." Tamia got up from the bed and gathered her articles of clothing.

Madame walked on her soft carpet toward her large bathroom to take a shower and make herself presentable. Behind her she heard Tamia fixing to leave and she turned around before the door was all the way shut.

"Tamia?"

"Yes, Madame?"

"I believe it is time for you to lose some weight."

With that she flicked her wrist, dismissing the woman, and shut her bathroom door.

Chapter 14

"Welcome to the Opulent Inn!"

A voice caught them all off guard and they whipped around in the tasteful lobby. A woman's heels clicked and clacked on the ground as she hurriedly made her way over to them.

"I'm so sorry," she said. "I wasn't expecting anyone to come through those doors in this storm so I snuck off for a break."

She was a very pretty young lady with yellow skin and blond hair. Her high ponytail was slicked down so well that Rhonnie didn't know where her skin ended and where her hair started. She raised her eyebrows and felt Ahli nudge her, already knowing what she was thinking. Ahli gave her sister a side eye as if telling her not to say anything rude.

"No, you're okay . . . Reiah," Ahli said, reading the girl's nametag. "We were just looking for a place to rest our heads for the night."

"Okay, great," Reiah said and pressed some buttons on her computer. "Give me one second."

While Rhonnie and Ahli stood at the counter, Brayland's back was turned to them so that he could give the place a complete once-over. It was strange to him that a place like this was sitting in the middle of nowhere. Usually the nearer you got to a hotel this luxurious there would be signs everywhere, but he didn't remember seeing any. Or maybe he just hadn't been paying attention. What also seemed strange was the fact that suddenly when Reiah showed up so had more workers dressed in the exact same tight pants and low-cut shirts, and they were all women. Not just women, beautiful women. Women who seemed out of place working for somebody's inn.

"Brayland!"

"Huh?" he said, turning around to see everyone's eyes on him.

"I just called your name three times!"

"My bad. I was in my own world."

"The women at the Opulent Inn seem to have that effect on people." Reiah winked at him and received a deadly stare from Ahli.

"Mmm," Rhonnie said, handing him a key.

"Me and NaNa are going to share a room, is that cool? You'll be right down the hall from us."

"A'ight," Brayland said, trying to hide his slight disappointment.

"Just go that way, and around that corner. You won't miss it."

"Room fifty-eight," Rhonnie said, reading the number on her key. "Come on, LaLa, I need some rest. Especially after you destroyed my car, knowing I'm broke now. And then tried to kill us."

Despite the situation Ahli grinned at the back of her sister's head and pretended to punch her.

"I'm in room sixty-two," Brayland said. "Hopefully it's not too far from y'all just in case I need to—"

"Need to what?" Rhonnie remarked over her shoulder. "Sneak in and save Ahli with your snake?"

"Rhonnie!"

"Hssss."

It was Brayland's turn to laugh when Rhonnie made a hissing sound at Ahli. He shook his head and winked at Ahli, making her face turn red.

"I can't stand either one of you!" she exclaimed and pushed past them both so that she could lead the way.

"I've been meaning to ask you something," Rhonnie said to Brayland when Ahli was out of earshot.

"What's good?"

"It's about the drugs Ahli and I stole a little while back."

"What about them?"

"You said they belonged to the Last Kings. Do you think it was them who killed Daddy?"

She'd been wanting to get him alone to ask him that question for a while now. However, with Ahli wanting to drop the whole "searching for his killer" thing, she knew she best not bring it up around her. She studied Brayland's face for an answer as they walked side by side.

"Honestly? Nah." Bray shook his head.

"Why not? You yourself said they were ruthless!"

"I said ruthless? Try merciless, try savage. Try—"

"Okay. I get your drift." She put her hand up to stop him from ranting. "But, exactly! If they are all of that then why don't you think they would do that to my father for what we did?"

"Because they would have finished the job." He nodded from her to Ahli. "They would have waited for you to get back to the house and killed you. I would bet money that they were the ones who killed Dot."

"How do you know?"

"Because that's what I would have done."

They reached his room before Rhonnie could say anything else. He used his key to open his door and looked down the hall to see Ahli doing the same thing. Their eyes connected and the smile they shared was enough; no words needed to be spoken. She opened her door and disappeared in the room.

"Do me a favor and make sure she's straight, a'ight?"

"That's my sister, stupid." Rhonnie rolled her eyes at him and walked away. "Just because you're her nigga or whatever you want to call it doesn't mean I'll stop being that."

He had half a mind to snatch her up by the still-wet ponytail on her head, but he didn't. He just chuckled to himself and let the door slam shut behind him.

"Damn," he said, looking around the room. It was fit for a king, with a circular king-sized bed in the middle of it. The carpet was cocaine white, so white it would make a person hesitant to walk on it. He took his shoes off at the door, not wanting to add carpet cleaning to their already high bill.

He removed the poncho and set it on one of the golden dressers so that he could fall backward on the thick red comforter. The bed was the softest thing his body had ever graced in his life. It was almost like he was lying on a cloud in the form of a bed. The room smelled of fresh linen and the fan above him was encrusted with diamonds. He couldn't help but wonder if they were real; and, if they were, that meant the inn saw some real money. The flat-screen TV practically covered the wall in front of the bed, and he couldn't wait to watch a movie on it.

"Damn," he said, thinking about how much more amazing the room would have been if Ahli were there with him.

With a sigh of disappointment he got up from the bed so that he could explore the room further. He went through the closets and, like in most hotels, he found a blow dryer, an iron with an ironing board, and extra towels. It wasn't until he started rummaging through the drawers that he saw something he'd never seen before.

Every drawer was filled with men's clothing, all brand new with the tags still attached. His eyebrow raised when he pulled a pair of Ralph Lauren boxers with the matching pajamas from the golden dresser. He looked around the room to make sure he wasn't being punk'd before he rubbed a hand over the blond tips on his fade.

"I'll leave 'em here," he told himself, wanting nothing more than to get out of the wet clothes he was wearing.

He tucked the clothes under his arm so that he could head to the bathroom and stay there for an hour. It had been awhile since he'd been alone and it was time for him to clear out his thoughts. There was nothing special about the bathroom besides its exceptionally large size and the fact that there was no tub, just a brick shower with an overhead showerhead.

This shit is crazy, he thought as he lathered his body up with the complimentary soap the inn offered. If anybody had told him two months ago that he would be in Nebraska in two months, not dealing drugs and in love, he would have knocked them out for lying.

In love?

He couldn't be in love, could he? He didn't think he was capable of that emotion, but the more he thought about it, the more he knew it was true. There was nothing else that would keep him in the situation he was currently in. There was nothing else that would have kept him boxed in such a small city. The only reason he stayed was because he couldn't imagine not being by Ahli, not until he knew what could be first. And now he knew, and he would never leave.

He smiled in the shower remembering her smile. Not the one with her sad eyes; her real smile, the one she gave him after they made love for the first time. His mind wandered off to the way her body jerked before she let go of her sea of love around his . . .

"Down, boy." He looked down at his erection, knowing there wouldn't be anything that he could do about it until after the job.

He finished his shower and wrapped a towel around his waist to go back into the bedroom area. He was almost finished getting dressed with his back to the door when he heard it open and close behind him. He smiled while he put the white T-shirt over his head, thinking that Ahli had snuck the extra key to his room.

"You miss me alre—"

His statement was cut short when he turned around and saw that it wasn't Ahli standing there in her underwear. It was a white woman he'd never seen in his life. He couldn't deny that she was beautiful, and that she had a nice body. It just wasn't the one he wanted to see. He figured she was somebody's girl who was staying at the inn and maybe she'd ventured into the wrong room.

"I think you're in the wrong room, lady," Brayland told her and put his hands up in the air. "Ain't nobody with a name like Tom here."

The woman smiled at his joke and cocked her head. She eyed him lustfully and licked her lips. "I'm not in the wrong room," her soft, sweet voice said with her hands behind her back. "I came here for you."

"Nah, ma," Brayland told her, stepping toward her. "You need to get the fuck out before my girl comes and beats your ass."

When he tried to push her away she stood on her tiptoes so that his hands would be forced to slide down to her breasts. Feeling them in his palms he hesitated.

"You like that, don't you?" she said, looking deeply into his face. "This is compliments of Madame. She wants me to show you a good time. So just let Diamond please you, baby. I can handle that for you."

On the word "that" she brought one of her hands from behind her back and stroked his erection. Her eyes brightened at his size and she dropped to her knees in hopes of deep-throating him until he released all over her face.

"I said nah, man." Brayland stepped back and pointed to the door. "Tell Madame or whoever, I'm straight. I don't need no ho service, or whatever you call yourself. Now get the fuck out. I just told your simple ass I got a girl."

Diamond had fire in her eyes when she stood. No man had ever denied her, especially when they were about to get her special treatment. He turned his back on her and waved her away with a flick of his wrist. Her nose flared and she brought the object that she had hiding behind her back to the front of her.

"A girl, huh? I hate to be the one to break it to you, but your girl is about to be dead. Just like you!"

"Wha—"

It was too late. Brayland turned back around to Diamond rushing him on the bed with a huge chef's knife.

"Die!"

When he fell back helplessly on the bed she brought the knife down on his chest, splattering the carpet with his blood.

Chapter 15

"How come every woman who works here looks like they could be on the cover of a magazine?" Rhonnie asked Ahli as she climbed into the bed beside her. "Even the ones mopping the floor had bodies better than the ones these industry hoes buy."

"Shut up, NaNa." Ahli giggled from where she sat up straight on the bed. "They weren't even that cute."

"Of course you say that, especially since Brayland was gawking at them."

"Brayland wasn't gawking at shit." Ahli pushed Rhonnie away from her with her feet until she was almost hanging off of the bed. "Take it back!"

"Stop!" Rhonnie shouted through her own fits of giggles.

"Take it back!" Ahli repeated.

"Okay! I take it back, I take it back! I'm about to fall off this tall-ass bed. Stop!"

Ahli allowed her to come back on the California king without issue but gave her a look as if to say "don't try me again." Both girls were in the bed clean and dry with black cotton shorts and white T-shirts they'd found in one of the drawers of the cozy room. At first Ahli was certain that she wouldn't be able to get any sleep that night, but after she took a long, hot shower and put on clothes that smelled like they'd come straight out of the dryer, she began to rethink the fact. She figured if she shut her eyes for some hours then the morning would come faster. And if it came faster that meant they could get to the money sooner, and that meant they could all try to get on with their lives.

Rhonnie scooted as close to her sister's warm body as she could. The bed was so comfortable that it seemed sleep was begging for her to find it. She was so soothed by the soft white pillow under her head that she didn't know how she was going to get up in the morning. Ahli and Brayland would have to pry her away from the bed, she was sure of it. There was something so familiar about the room but she couldn't put her finger on it. Her eyes were certain they hadn't been laid on anything in the room prior to them staying there, and she knew for a fact that she'd never been there before.

"It smells just like Mommy in here," Ahli whispered, interrupting Rhonnie's thoughts and lying back onto the bed. She placed her arms under her pillow and held it to her face so that she could breathe in the smell. "Don't you think so?"

That's it, Rhonnie thought. *It smells just like Mommy.* "You're right," Rhonnie said, turning over on her stomach so that she could bury her head in the fluffy white pillow.

It had been so long since their noses had been blessed with the earthy yet floral aroma that belonged to Rhebecca, and both girls wanted to relish the scent. It was almost as if she was in the room with them. They were both so caught up in living in the past that neither felt themselves drifting off, due to the chloroform that drenched the inside cotton of the pillows.

"Ahli, go help your sister get down!"

An eight-year-old Ahli smacked her lips before looking apologetically at the friends she'd just made at the park. She then ran to where her sister was stuck, only to see that she wasn't even stuck. She was

*frozen at the top of the fire pole with her feet still
planted safely on the jungle gym while her little hands
were clamped around the pole. Ahli kicked the sand
with her Reeboks in a tantrum before running back
to where her mother sat on a bench watching her
daughters play.*

*"I thought I told you to get NaNa." Rhebecca raised
her eyebrow at her oldest child. The wind blew her
long, freshly straightened hair, so she tucked it behind
her ears on both sides. She noticed Ahli's jacket wasn't
zipped all the way, even though she made sure it
was zipped all the way up to her neck before they'd left
the house.*

*"LaLa, do you want to get sick?" She pulled Ahli close
to her so that she could zip her coat up once again.
"What have I told you about running around in this
chilly weather with an open coat?"*

*"But, Mommy! None of the other kids wear their
jackets zipped up like this! Only babies do, like Rhonnie."
Ahli stuck her tongue out and pointed her finger toward
her throat like she wanted to barf.*

*"Stop it." Rhebecca couldn't help but smile at the rebel
burning deep inside her daughter's heart. "I don't care
what these other kids are doing. I'm not their mama.
You'll thank me one day when they're in the hospital
dying of pneumonia. And, speaking of your sister, I
thought I told you to go help her."*

*"Mommy, she's not even stuck. She's just scared on the
fire pole again! When I was six I loved going down
the fire pole! What is she so scared of? And all the kids
keep laughing at her."*

*"When you were six you had your father to help you
down the pole." Rhebecca stared into the eyes that
mirrored her own down to the light brown specks in
them. "That little girl has you. Now, I don't know if*

you've been acting out because your father is gone or if it's because you need the attention of someone who thinks the world of you. If that's the case, you have that in that little girl standing there, watching her big sister pay attention to everyone else but the person whose whole life revolves around her. Have you ever thought about why she even goes to that pole? Did you ever once think that it's because she sees you slide down it so effortlessly?"

Ahli turned away from her mother and looked behind her to where her sister still stood frozen in the same spot. That time, however, she paid attention to her face. She looked like she was trying to will herself to do something that she just couldn't; and it didn't make things better that the other kids were taunting her.

Her mother gripped her chin and forced Ahli to look at her again. "Listen to me, baby. That's your sister, your little sister. You only get one. There will come a day when all you two have is each other. Love your sister, honor your sister, and most of all don't let anyone hurt your sister. That includes her feelings, too."

Ahli sighed and tried to hide the fact that she felt like the absolute scum of the universe, but that didn't go unnoticed by Rhebecca. She hugged Ahli tightly to her and kissed her lovingly on her forehead.

"Go on now. Be the good big sis I know you can be. And when we get home I'll teach you how to play Vita."

"Promise?" Ahli's entire mood brightened at the mention of her mother's piano.

"Promise!"

Ahli broke away from Rhebecca and ran back toward the jungle gym. She climbed the stairs and crossed the bridge until she was standing behind Rhonnie.

"Hurry up and go down, freak!" a cruel little boy with freckles and red hair said to her. "There are other kids who want to play on the fire pole, doo-doo head!"

"Hey!" Ahli yelled, getting in the kid's face. "Don't talk to my sister like that or I'm going to bust your head to the white meat!"

The boy's eyes widened when the older kid yelled at him and he instantly backed off. He and his friends ran off to go down the winding slide, leaving Ahli alone with her sister. Rhonnie had a surprised look on her cute six-year-old face.

"Thanks, Ahli," she said and looked down at the purple Chuck Taylors on her feet. "I'm sorry I'm such a scaredy-cat freak."

Ahli felt bad that Rhonnie felt that way, especially knowing that she had helped make her feel that way. She couldn't help it; she stepped forward and grabbed her little sister and hugged her tight. She didn't know how she could ever have been so mean to someone who looked so much like her.

"I'm sorry, NaNa," she said. "You're not a freak. You're the coolest kid I know and I'm never going to be mean to you again. I promise!"

"Even when I play with your dolls?"

"They're our dolls now," Ahli told her when she let her go. "But only if you go down the fire pole."

"But it's so far down! What if I let go and fall?"

Ahli shrugged her shoulders. "Just make sure you land on your feet then."

Rhonnie still looked terrified at first but Ahli's bright grin made it subside. She looked back at the blue fire pole and then back at her big sister.

"Okay, I'll do it," she said and went back to the pole. She wrapped her hands and one leg around it and prepared to push herself from the edge of the jungle

gym. Before she launched herself in a spiral downward motion she looked back at Ahli. "Do you love me, Ahli?"

Ahli's brow furrowed at the fact that Rhonnie would even ask her that. Although Rhonnie could be an annoying little sister she wanted her to know she was always loved. That was something that would never change. "Always and forever, NaNa," she said seriously and then grinned again. "Now go! Mommy said she's going to show me how to play her piano later and you know she doesn't let anyone touch it! I'll make up a song for you since you haven't been able to sleep lately."

"Okay, cool!" Rhonnie kicked herself from the jungle gym and squealed with glee the whole way down.

"You did it!" Ahli yelled down at Rhonnie who was jumping up and down.

"Mommy, I did it!" Rhonnie yelled to her mother, who was standing up and smiling with a hand over her chest. "Ahli, I love you! Always and forever!"

"Always and forever."

The sound of dripping water brought Ahli out of her dream. It seemed so real. She could still feel her mother's warm embrace and the sand slipping inside of her shoes.

"Always and forever," she said again. Her voice came out in a groggy tone and her body felt like she had been hit with a ton of bricks. Ahli expected to wake up in the same soft bed she'd fallen asleep in, except she didn't remember falling asleep. Her head kept falling forward, making her chin hit her chest with each uncontrollable nod.

"Ahli!"

She recognized the voice, but it sounded so far away. With some difficulty she tried to open her eyes, but her vision was blurred. She tried to rub her eyes but every time she tried to move her arms, she couldn't.

"Ahli!"

"Rhonnie?" Although her head felt heavy, Ahli used all the energy she could to lift it up and turn it the way she heard the voice. Blinking feverishly she was able to clear her sight, but she wasn't able to get rid of the throbbing headache that she had. What she saw confused her and made her want to get to where her sister was sitting.

"W . . . what's going on?" she asked. "Why are you tied to a chair?

She looked down at her own arms and saw that she too was bound by brown rope to a wooden chair. She didn't understand what was happening; surely she was still dreaming. She tried to shut her eyes again but, of course, she was already truly roused. No longer was she smelling the sweet scent of her mother; instead, there was a tart odor disrespecting her nostrils.

"She chloroformed us! The pillows, Ahli. She knocked us out."

The longer her eyes were open the more in tune she became with her surroundings. They were in some sort of room. The lights were dim there but she was able to make out objects around the room. Most of it was junk, things nobody wanted anymore, and boxes. To the far right she saw what looked to be five white bags, and to her far left she was able to see one window with a box under it. By the way the window was angled she knew that they were underground somewhere.

"Who are you talking about, Rhonnie? Who is 'she'?"

"Me," a baleful voice spoke.

Ahli whipped her head in the direction of the voice and saw the silhouette of a woman. She too was sitting in a chair, except hers was in front of the only door in the room, facing them. Her upper half was completely concealed by the shadows of the room but Ahli could make out the Lady Peep Louis Vuitton shoes on her feet. Her legs were crossed and her leg on top of the other shook, like she'd been standing by for something to happen.

"I've been waiting for you to wake up, my dear Ahli," she said. "It's a pleasure to finally meet the two of you. After all, you have me to thank for your existence."

"What are you talking about?" Ahli said and began to fight against her restraints, but it was no use. Whoever tied them up was a professional. "What kind of sick game are you playing at? Let us go!"

"Yes, just let us go," Rhonnie tried to beg. "We have a job tomorrow and with the kind of money we're getting we can pay you whatever you want!"

There was a pause before they heard an omniscient laugh coming from where she perched in the shadows. "That's right," the voice said. "You think you have a job, don't you? Let me be the first to tell you that you don't. It was all a setup, to get you here."

Rhonnie's eyes grew as big as saucers and her mouth dropped open while Ahli glared at the figure.

"Who are you?" Ahli demanded. "What the fuck do you want? Why do you have us tied down here like some fucking animals?"

"Me? I am your worst nightmare. And I want your souls."

Her response sent chills down Ahli's spine. It was then she knew she was in the presence of the grim reaper herself.

"Are you two familiar with what happens when a loved one dies and they have balances left unpaid? It goes to the next of kin."

"We don't know anybody who knows you," Rhonnie growled. "Let us go!"

"Are you stupid, or are you dumb?" the woman snapped so ferociously that Rhonnie almost bit her tongue. "Do you think I went through all of the trouble to get you down here just to let you go?"

She laughed again and uncrossed her legs. Both sisters sat up straight in their seats when she stood up from her chair.

"I would have expected more from Rhebecca's children."

Hearing her mother's name shocked Ahli. She scrunched her face up and tried to force her eyes to see past the darkness and into the assailant's face. "How do you know my mother?"

"Rhebecca? She was one of my best girls; that is, until that man came and stole her away. I never saw her again, and she stole something that I want. Something that I need, and you two are going to tell me where it is."

Her heels were loud in the quiet, musty room with each step she took forward. She wore a sleek black dress, as if she were going to a funeral, and her long jet-black hair hung freely around her face. Her face was so smooth that Ahli couldn't tell if she was a natural beauty or if she had makeup on her face. Either way she was the most gorgeous woman Ahli had ever seen in her life. The red lipstick on the woman's lips resembled blood and she had something in her hand that gleamed in the light of the one light bulb. Ahli wasn't able to make it out until the woman was closer to her. The machete was long and freshly sharpened, like she had prepared for this very moment.

"What are you going to do with that?"

"Exactly what Anna here did to your father. After I told her to, of course. Come here, Anna. Now!"

She pointed to somebody behind Ahli and she tried to turn her head around, but she didn't need to. The pretty golden brown–skinned woman they met earlier stepped around where Ahli's chair was. Except that time the only clothes she wore were lingerie.

"You killed my daddy?" Rhonnie asked incredulously, staring at the woman who had given them all a ride in the rain. "You killed my daddy!"

Rhonnie fought so hard against the ropes on her arms that her wrists began to bleed. Ahli, on the other hand, felt like somebody punched her in the gut. Something her father told her made its way back to her frontal lobe and something clicked.

"You're Madame," she said finally, with tears in her eyes. She took an unsteady breath and looked to Anna and back to the woman in the black dress. "Aren't you?"

"I see my reputation precedes me," Madame said with a sickening smile. "Tell them, Anna. Tell them what you did."

"I killed him," Anna whispered, stating the fact of the matter. Her voice was monotone and she relived the last moments of Quinton's life. "I rang the doorbell and he answered, not knowing that I was going to be the one to slit his throat. He made me so mad. He wouldn't talk. No matter how many times I stabbed him, he wouldn't talk. He didn't tell me anything that I needed to know, so I slice his throat out. Since he wouldn't tell me what I wanted, I made sure he could never talk again."

Rhonnie's breathing was rigid, but she'd used all her energy to do any more fighting. She felt helpless.

When she looked into Ahli's eyes, her big sister saw something she never thought she'd see again in them. Defeat.

"You, my dears, are in the Opulent Inn, where my girls can either fulfill your every desire, or make every nightmare you've ever had come true. Whatever I tell them to do, they do. Except Rhebecca, she is the only girl who left me. She was disobedient and ungrateful. I took her from the streets and gave her a home!"

"You made her a sex slave!" Ahli screamed. "You took away any ability she had at making a choice of her own! That's why she ran. That's why she left!"

"And that's why you're here!" Madame snarled and swung the machete at Ahli's neck, stopping abruptly right before it connected. "You both will be repaying her debt. She stole something from me, and you both are going to tell me where it is."

"We don't know what you want!" Rhonnie's eyes were frozen on how close the blade was to her sister's neck.

"Oh, but you do. Or, at least, she does." Madame leered down at Ahli. "Come on, Ahli, tell Madame where it is."

"Where what is?"

"The formula!"

The formula? Ahli thought until it clicked in her head. *The formula!* "I don't know what you're talking about."

But it was too late. Madame had already seen in her eyes that she knew what she was talking about. She placed the blade on Ahli's collarbone and cut her deeply. Rhonnie gritted her teeth, trying to stomach the pain, but it didn't work. The scream still seeped through her lips.

"Now we can be twins." Madame pointed to her own neck. "Do you both want to know how I got this? I was eighteen, fresh out of high school, and walking home. I went the route that I took every day, but I guess that didn't work in my favor. Somebody had been watching me, a group of someones, actually. They surrounded me in an alley, told me they liked how my titties bounced when I walked. They held me down and one of them held a machete to my neck while the others copped feels all over my body. They stuck their fingers in all my holes and taunted me, telling me that the only reason they were doing it was because they could. They told me that pussy ran the world and so they wanted some of mine.

"I was still a virgin, and that was stripped from me by a dirty man and his friends. My neck jerked while they were violating me and the machete cut my neck deep; a little more to the left and my throat would have been sliced open. The blood must have scared the one holding the machete, because he dropped it and the person holding my arms down let me go too. I grabbed the machete and started hacking away. I killed all of them, and then chopped their dicks off."

Ahli couldn't even begin to feel sorry for the woman before her. She was the one responsible for her father's death. "If that happened to you why do you have women as sexual weapons?"

"Because pussy runs the world. I learned then that men will do unethical things for pussy. I realized then that men are weak and now I control them. Every woman here is a woman I saved from what happened to me and I prevented it from happening to them. Now they know the power that they have. Now they know that they can get whatever they want from a man."

"But what about from you?" Rhonnie asked. "You're so busy trying to control them that you don't even realize that you've become the thing you claim you're trying to protect your so-called girls from. You're a monster!"

"But they call me Madame." Madame shrugged. "Once I get that formula I will become even more powerful. Not only will I have a drug that nobody else has even come close to creating, but I will have dominance over the world. Both men and women will bow to me, and the Opulent Inn will expand to many more places. I will have influence everywhere."

"You're sick."

"No." Madame turned her back on them and looked at Anna. "You're going to be sick if you don't tell Anna where the formula is. I'm giving you thirty minutes. Fifteen minutes each. Make it hurt."

"Yes, Madame."

"Wait! Where is Brayland?" Ahli asked. "The guy I came with?"

Madame turned around and smirked at the sweaty girl who looked so much like her favorite girl. "I had no use for him. He's dead," she said and left the room.

Chapter 16

Anna got straight to business as soon as Madame left. All she wanted to do was please her and remain in her good graces. If all she had to do was cause others pain so in turn she would not feel any, why not? She thought back to when she traveled to Quinton. She didn't know why she had been so scared to hurt him at first. After all, it was just a little blood. Gone was that frightened girl who tried to run away from it all. Her mind was clear, more like empty, but still she was able to see everything clearly now. When she looked down at Rhonnie and Ahli, she didn't see two helpless women tied to a chair. She saw the enemy, an enemy who needed to be punished for not giving Madame what she wanted, so she made them scream. Starting with Rhonnie.

"Where is it?"

"I keep telling you I don't—"

Anna sliced her in the side with the machete that Madame left her.

"Hssss! Ahhhhhh!" Rhonnie clenched her eyes shut and yelled out.

"Stop lying! Where did Quinton put it?"

"I don't know!"

Once again, Anna didn't like the answer that she was given. Not once did she think that maybe Rhonnie was telling the truth. If Madame said they knew, then they knew. She hauled off and punched Rhonnie in her face, causing a sickening thud and throwing Rhonnie's head to the right. When Rhonnie tried to turn her face back Anna punched her again, harder. And again, and again.

"Stop it! I'm going to fucking kill you, bitch! Get the fuck away from her!" Ahli fought against the ropes on her arms and legs and made her chair shake violently. Her head was still pounding from the drug, but seeing the blood coming from Rhonnie's nose and her side was giving her all the adrenaline she needed.

"Rhonnie!" Ahli screamed and watched as Anna continued to use her sister's body as a punching bag and a carving tool. "You stupid-ass bitch! He didn't tell her. He told me!"

"Love your sister, honor your sister, and most of all don't let anyone hurt your sister."

Rhebecca's voice snuck into Ahli's mind and she did the only thing she could to save her sister. It worked because instantly Anna whipped around and took a few steps to get to her. She placed the blade on Ahli's already open wound and applied pressure. It hurt but if Anna thought the pain was what was causing the tears to fall from her eyes, she was mistaken. Ahli's gaze was straight forward and on her sister. If she hadn't been tied to the chair she was sure Rhonnie would have passed out on the floor. It looked like she was trying to get a grip on herself, but the trauma to her face was causing her to nod in and out of consciousness.

"Then where is it?" Anna punched Ahli hard in the mouth with her knuckles. "If you don't tell me, Madame will do much worse to you than what I did to her."

When Ahli hesitated she pressed on Ahli's wound even harder and blood trickled down the white shirt she was wearing. Ahli's lip stung and the pain in her neck was something she'd never felt in her life, but it wasn't until she looked into Anna's eyes that she realized she would never know what true pain was.

"She doesn't love you," Ahli told her, spitting blood to the side. "She owns you. There is a difference."

"Shut up. You don't know anything about Madame!"

"I don't know how many of you killer hoes there are here, but from the size of this building there must be a lot of you. I know that right now, at any second, any one of you could wise up and run. Just like my mother did."

"Your mother was a traitor!" Anna dropped the machete to the ground and grabbed a fistful of Ahli's hair. She straddled her and got so close to Ahli that she could see the pores in her skin. "She disobeyed Madame and now her entire family is paying for it! Do you know Quinton begged me to spare your lives? He begged me not to lay a finger on you two." She threw her head back and gave a hearty laugh.

"Maybe you're right, but one thing she never was, was a traitor. She did something none of you other bitches have the balls to do. The only thing keeping you here is fear. There are no locks on your doors, no shackles on your feet."

"She will kill us all if we run! She will always find us!"

"She never found my mother, and she only found us by chance." Ahli smirked at Anna and nodded to all the cuts on her body. "Aw, did she slice that mentality into you? Sounds a lot like what masters do to their slaves, slave."

Her words jarred a memory in Anna's head. Her taunts touched her in a place that had been dead and gone for so long. The place that had caused her to run when she had first gotten to the Opulent Inn, the hopeful place. She let go of Ahli's hair and looked down at her own hands. Turning her head around she looked at Rhonnie's bludgeoned body and felt a rush of remorse.

"But Madame, she saved me. Sh . . . she took me in."

"And never let you leave." Ahli saw that she was getting through to her. When Quinton was telling her about the place that her mother came from, he told her that most of the women were incapable of thinking for themselves. That the place was equivalent to a cult and Madame was the head of it. Ahli didn't know how to feel for Anna, but she knew that if she could maybe open her eyes then she had a chance at saving Rhonnie's life.

"Do you know what she will be able to do if she gets the formula to that drug? My mother ran away because she understood; now I'm going to make you understand. She will force you all to take this drug, and she will force you to stay on it. She has already gotten inside of your mind with fear, but you still have a choice no matter if you think you do or not. This drug will take away your choice. Not only will she own you, but you might as well call yourselves Madame too because all you will be is an extension of her in an empty shell. Imagine all of the women she will taint. Imagine the money and power she will gain around the world. What do you think someone like that will do with complete domination? You can kill us now, but you might as well kill yourself too."

Anna's eyes glossed over and she looked into Ahli's eyes trying to find dishonesty, but she couldn't. She didn't see any. She jumped to her feet when she heard the sound of a vibrating phone coming from behind Ahli's chair, where she originally was when the girls came to. She picked up her machete and went to answer it.

"Yes, Madame." She paused for a moment. "No, neither of them are talking." She paused again. "Okay." She hung up the phone and turned back to where the girls were strapped to the chairs. Rhonnie was still nodding off and Ahli was beginning to lose too much blood from her neck.

"I told you," Anna whispered. "I told you that if you didn't talk she would hurt you far worse than what I could. It is time to go to Madame's quarters."

Chapter 17

When Anna untied her, Ahli wanted nothing more than to fight her off and rescue her sister. She wanted to snatch the machete from Anna's hand and give her a taste of her own medicine. But when she stood, she collapsed. She'd lost too much blood and she was losing control of her body. The room around her began to fade to black and she knew that she was about to be reunited with her mother and father.

Anna untied Rhonnie and forced her to her feet.

"Ahli?" she moaned. When she got no response she began to sob. "Ahli!"

Her sister was lying on the ground of the cold room with blood dripping from her neck. She looked lifeless and Rhonnie tried to focus her eyesight on Ahli's chest to see if it was moving even in the slightest bit.

"Help her walk." Anna pointed the blade in Rhonnie's direction. "Or I will make you immobile just like her."

Rhonnie didn't need to be told twice. The aftereffect of the drugs and the trauma to her head made everything a blur, but she pushed through to kneel down unsteadily. Placing a shaky finger under Ahli's nostrils, Rhonnie stopped breathing herself and stood still to see if she felt her sister's breath. When she felt the warm air on her finger she felt relief, but she knew that if she moved Ahli the blood flow coming from the wound would quicken.

"I need something to stop the bleeding," Rhonnie said and looked around. She scrunched up her face from the throbbing in both of her temples. Her vision would blur and then come back into focus, but she didn't stop scanning the large room. Along the white brick walls were many things, like old furniture and other trinkets, but no cloth.

"I need something for her neck! Whatever you want, she knows it. Whatever you need, she's the only one who can help you find it!"

Anna still stood over them, seemingly unmoved until Rhonnie pointed to the corner.

"There! Rip that cloth so I can put it around her neck."

She'd pointed to the corner to where the white bags were and Anna followed her finger.

"Those are dead bodies," she said emotionlessly. "The customers I killed to ensure that you two wouldn't suspect anything."

Rhonnie's stomach turned at the thought of putting the cloth on Ahli's open lesion, but she didn't have a choice. "Rip it, or she dies. And Madame never gets the formula."

Anna hesitated at first. The only person she took orders from was Madame, but seeing Ahli bleeding out she knew Madame would be upset if she let the girl die. She went to where the bodies were. Touching one of the bags she felt that it was still warm, being as it had been a corpse only for a couple of hours. She rolled it over, preparing to cut the cloth, but that side was covered in blood. She'd forgotten that she slit all of their necks, so she was forced to cut the cloth by their back. Using the machete she slit a piece long enough to fold and wrap around Ahli's neck.

"Hurry up," Anna said, handing her the piece of fabric. "Madame does not like to wait."

Rhonnie took it and folded it so that it would provide a thicker comfort. She then gently raised Ahli's head so that she could tie it around her neck tightly, but not so tight that she would choke.

"LaLa." Rhonnie smacked her sister's face to get her eyes to open. "I'm going to help you walk, but you have to help me back, okay?"

Ahli's eyes rolled to the back of her head, but she heard her sister speak. She weakly nodded right before she felt Rhonnie hoist her to her feet. Their legs were shaky, but by leaning on each other they were able to get a firm footing.

"When I use my right leg, use your left, okay?" Rhonnie panted into Ahli's ear. "I'm not going to let you fall, sister."

"The elevator is down the hall." Anna opened the door for them to go through and watched them struggle through the door and down the long hallway. When one slid, the other would muster the strength to pull her back up. Anna knew from personal experience how they felt. She reflected on the nights that she was severely punished. The many nights she was forced to sleep on bloody sheets while the gashes in her back bled out. She remembered not being able to move, even if she tried to will herself. She was beaten until she submitted to Madame's will. Madame literally beat obedience into her, like a slave.

She broke me, Anna thought once they were on the elevator. *She is my master.*

The elevator let them off right down the hall from Madame's room. Mentally she was somewhere else; her body was working on its own accord. It knew where it was going, but she didn't remember actually getting there. She knocked quietly on the door, holding the machete up as if to let the girls know not to pull any funny business, and waited for Madame to open the door.

"I called you fifteen minutes ago." Madame glowered past the two women and at Anna. "You should have been here twelve minutes ago."

Anna pushed the women through the doorway, where they promptly buckled to the soft carpet in the vast room. Both girls heaved in and out, being as they had used most of their energy walking to the room. Ahli had gained some of her consciousness back. Rhonnie tied the cloth around her neck tight enough to slow the bleeding tremendously. Still, if she didn't seek medical attention soon, the results would be fatal.

Wrapping her arms around her sister, Rhonnie hoisted Ahli into a sitting position between her legs. She scooted them backward until her back was on the wall by the door.

"Oh my God. Ahli, look," Rhonnie whispered into Ahli's hair, ignoring the sting on her busted lips from her sister's hair products. "Look on the bed."

Rhonnie knew the exact moment that Ahli took notice of what she was talking about, because she felt her body tense up. *How did we get here?* Rhonnie asked herself. *How could we fall into a trap like this? Daddy taught us better.*

"They could barely walk, Madame," Anna answered Madame. "I had to wait for them to get here."

"Then you should have dragged them!" Madame replied icily. "If you would have done your job correctly then they wouldn't have had to come here! You incompetent puppet!"

Anna's jaw tensed, but she didn't say anything. She just fixed her face before Madame took notice of it. She watched Madame strut happily to her bed and it was at that moment that Anna noticed the things strewn all over her bed. Torture weapons. From knives to guns to syringes filled with only God knew what.

"Let's have some fun." Madame ran her freshly painted nails over all of the instruments on the bed. "Which one do you two want to play with?"

She spun around to where Ahli and Rhonnie were huddled against the wall. Her eyes darted from Rhonnie to Ahli and then back to Rhonnie. There was a twinkle in her eyes and she slowly lifted her pointer finger to them. "I choooose," she said in a sing-song voice, moving her finger back and forth like she was playing Eeny Meeny Miny Moe. "You!"

Her finger stopped on Ahli and her dark grin became a full-blown malicious laugh when she witnessed Rhonnie's hold on her tighten.

"You're about to die anyway." She made a face and patted her own neck. "I think I cut you too deep. I need to pick your brain before I give your soul to the devil." From the bed she grabbed three small knives and placed them between her fingers.

"Stay away from us! Or—"

"Or you'll what? End up sliced up like your father?" Madame leered at her. "Now, you're going to tell me everything you know about *Vita E Morte*. Now! Where is the formula?"

"Go to hell," Ahli said weakly. "Even if I knew where it was I would never tell you. Bitch."

"So be it," Madame told her and progressed toward her, imagining herself slicing her pretty little lips off. However, another thought came to mind and she stopped to smile cunningly down at her. "I know how to make you talk. Anna, come here, and bring your toy."

"Yes, Madame?" Anna asked her when she was standing side by side next to the taller woman.

"I changed my mind," Madame said, looking dead into Ahli's eyes. "I only need one of them for now. Kill the younger one and make *her* watch."

"No!" Ahli raised her arms to protect her little sister from the machete. Her eyes pleaded with Anna. "Please. Stop letting her control you! She doesn't care about you, or any of them. She only cares about herself. What has she really done for you?"

"Anna! Kill her!"

"Anna, kill her," Ahli mimicked. "Do you ever think for yourself, Anna? Or does Madame do that for you, too? Don't you see why she can't get her hands on that drug?"

"Anna kill her! Now!"

"No, please," Ahli pleaded.

"Shut up!" Anna screamed at the top of her lungs. She brought her hands to her ears, trying to get a grip on herself.

Madame smirked. "Right," she said. "Shut up, Ahli, and prepare to watch your sister bleed dry in front of you knowing that it was all your fault."

"Actually, I was talking to you." Anna turned on Madame and held the machete in both hands in front of her. "You will not hurt anyone else ever again!"

Madame was shocked to say the least, but she regained her composure almost instantly. The blade was centimeters from her face; all Anna had to do was swing once. Madame looked into Anna's angry face and, even though she was threatening her life, all she saw was a scared little girl. Madame stared without blinking into Anna's eyes and moved her face closer to the machete.

"I always thought Rhebecca was my biggest disappointment, but it was you. I saved you! When you were alone and nobody wanted you, I took you! And this is the repayment I get? I should have killed you when I had the chance. Go ahead, do it." She stuck her tongue out and slowly licked the tip of the sharp object. "Kill me if you have the balls to do it. Kill me. Kill meeee!"

Anna's body shook and her face was twisted up as the saline tears fell down the sides of her face. "I hate you," she said, squeezing the handle of the weapon even tighter. "You didn't save me. You brought me to hell."

Anna brought her arms up with the weapon so that she could bring it down with force on Madame's neck. When Anna's arms went up so did the hand in which Madame had the small knives between her knuckles. She uppercut Anna repeatedly under her chin, until Anna's eyes looked like they were about to bulge through her head from choking on her own blood. When Madame drew her arm back the last time Anna's body dropped, jerking violently, to the ground. The skin underneath her chin was shredded, along with the bottom of her mouth and her tongue. When her eyes rolled to the back of her head and it was clear that she was dead, the only thing Madame felt remorseful about was her bloodstained carpet.

Madame turned back to where the girls had been huddled on the wall, intending to finish the job that Anna couldn't, only to find that they weren't there. The door to her room was wide open and she knew that when her attention was averted they must have made a run for it.

"This should be fun," she said and bent down to where Anna's dead body had fallen.

She grabbed the machete, the same one that had started all of this so long ago, and walked out of the room to find her two new additions. The only sounds that could be heard were the sounds of her heels stabbing the ground, and the calm humming coming from her mouth.

Chapter 18

"Come on, LaLa," Rhonnie panted, trying to make her sister keep up. "We have to get out of here before that psycho bitch kills us."

"We can't leave Brayland."

"You heard her; he's dead! And if we don't find a way out of here we're going to be dead too."

Ahli's heart was broken. She was positive that maybe she just wasn't meant to love. It hurt even more because she knew that Brayland's death was in her hands. If only he would have gone his separate way after fleeing Miami he would still be alive.

They moved as fast as they could through the long hallways of the Opulent Inn, hoping they wouldn't run into any more of Madame's puppets. The moment she had taken her eyes off of them they used that as their window of opportunity. She had been so thrown off by Anna's betrayal that she'd forgotten the real reason they were all in her room in the first place.

The girls hobbled down the hallway, struggling to move fast. They used each other and the walls on the sides of them for support and willed themselves to move forward, trying the doorknobs of every room they passed for refuge. Everything was locked and finally the pain was too much to bare.

"NaNa." Ahli stopped to lean on the wall. "I need a break."

Rhonnie looked behind them down the long, dimly lit hallway. No one had come yet, and all of the room doors were closed; still, she could only allow Ahli to rest for a minute. She rubbed her sister's back lovingly.

"I don't know how we got here. I can only guess that it's because of our parents." She sniffled and allowed herself to cry. "If I don't get the chance to tell you this ever again, I love you, Ahli. You are my best friend."

Ahli placed her palm over her little sister's bruised-up cheek and used her thumb to wipe one of the tears away. "I love you too, sister, and I'm sorry I wasn't able to protect you. I was supposed to protect you!"

"You've done a great job at doing that my whole life." Rhonnie grabbed Ahli's arm and put it over her shoulders. "Now it's my turn to return the favor."

In the distance they heard the sound of heels walking along the wooden floors echoing on the walls. Rhonnie got a good hold of Ahli before she began walking as fast as she could with Ahli in tow.

"I think the lobby is this way," she gasped. "We just need to get out of the doors and back to the highway so we can flag somebody down."

She held on to the hope that they were close to the exit, but at every turn instead of seeing the light from the lobby they were greeted with another hallway. She was going based off of a the faint memory of when they first walked in the building. She grew more and more discouraged but after a few more turns down dimly lit hallways they finally made it back to the brightly lit lobby. Time seemed to be on their side as there was no one at the front desk to stop them.

"Come on, sister, we are almost there."

The closer they got to the door, the more hope penetrated their chests. When they reached the doors Rhonnie reached for one of the handles and pulled.

"What's taking so long?" Ahli asked when the door didn't come open.

"I . . . I think it's locked!" Rhonnie exclaimed and removed Ahli's arm from around her neck so that she could help her sit down. She needed to use all of her strength to pull the door.

Even when she used both hands to pull and push at the doors, they wouldn't budge. They were trapped inside. "No!" Rhonnie screamed with sobs in her throat. "No, no, no!"

She banged at the doors in hope that maybe somebody on the outside would hear her. If only she had her gun then none of this would have taken place, but all of the weapons had been with Brayland.

"Silly girls." They heard the same cold voice as before come from behind them. "Did you really think that it would be that easy?"

When Rhonnie turned around she saw not only Madame, but at least twenty other women, half naked, holding sharp objects, standing around her in the huge lobby. All of them had a hungry look in their eyes.

Ahli had lost all the fight in her and the wound in her neck had started to bleed again. She was losing the feeling in her body and her vision began to come and go.

"What do you want from us? We don't have what you want!"

"Maybe not," Madame said and looked Rhonnie up and down. "But because of you I lost one of my best girls. I think I'll take the two of you as retribution. If you come without a struggle then I will see to it that Ahli gets the best medical treatment there is. She looks like she's, well, dying."

Rhonnie's eyes darted back to Ahli and she saw that she had fallen to the ground and was hopelessly clutching the cloth on her neck. She ran to her and dropped down to her knees to pick her sister's head up and hug it to her chest.

"No, Ahli," Rhonnie whined as she rocked back and forth. "Please don't leave me. Please don't leave me."

"If you don't come without a struggle then my girls will have no problem cutting you to shreds . . . literally."

Rhonnie held her sister close to herself and weighed her options. If she said yes then Ahli would live, but at what cost to them? To be forced to give their bodies night after night to complete strangers and never see the outside of that inn again unless Madame allowed it? That was no life, and Ahli would never forgive her if Rhonnie agreed to it, even if it meant saving their lives. Rhonnie spat toward them all and turned her nose up at them in a disgusted manner.

"Fuck you," Rhonnie told her, "and your hoes too. I'd rather die than to serve a monster."

"So be it."

Madame made no move except a slight gesture with her hand. The women recognized the kill signal, swarmed the girls, and began to slice away. Rhonnie covered her sister's body so that she would take all of the damage and pain. Her blood sprayed the walls of the lobby like new paint and her shrieks were equivalent to the ones you'd hear at an opera. Just when she was about to succumb to death she swore she heard the loud booming of the doors behind her being kicked open. Not only that but she swore she heard the sound of automatic rounds occupy the room, followed by screams and the sounds of bodies collapsing. Suddenly all the pain stopped, but she wasn't able to keep her eyes open long enough to see why. Karma had a funny way of coming back around. For her, it was with death.

Epilogue

Beep. Beep. Beep. Beep.

The sound of the machines hooked to the girls' bodies proved that there still was life in them. Sadie watched them both, waiting for one of them to come to. It had been a long two months, but finally she had tracked down the two people who had hit one of her most notorious trap houses in Omaha, Nebraska. The spot was so low and almost impenetrable so when she heard that it only took two people to rob her out of her product she was insulted. Now to find out that the two people were women, she was intrigued.

At first she thought Dot had robbed her since the product was recovered in his camp; however, when his dead body showed up more questions came up. She tied his men up by the ankles and shot off their toes one by one until they told her that he'd purchased the drugs from some man named Quinton. It wasn't too hard finding out where Quinton lived, especially since he made the rookie mistake of registering for the hotel he stayed in under his real name and address. Not only that but she realized that he'd become too comfortable when she and her men pulled up to his house preparing for a miniature war only to see him being removed from the house dead and on a stretcher. She recognized the team cleaning up the mess as one she often hired for the messy cleanups of her shooters in the city of Omaha. The fact that they shared the same connections intrigued her even more.

She took it upon herself to go inside and rummage through the house, knowing that she didn't trust any eyes but her own. She didn't find anything but a few old family pictures until she went inside of his room. There lay an artillery room behind an illusion bookshelf. She only saw it because whoever emptied it left the door slightly open.

She felt like Sherlock Holmes when she had her men scoop up the shattered pieces of the computer on the floor. She planned to figure out who had been bold enough to rob the Last Kings and put a whole clip in their skulls, especially since she was always just missing them in passing. When her best men finally cracked into the hard drive she had to admit that she was slightly astonished by the fact that the people who had hit her house were hired thieves. Thieves like Robin Hood, not the ones roaming the streets looking for a quick fix or come up.

She made her men dig deeper into the encoded files in the hard drive and soon they found where the next hit would be: Coralville, Iowa. She made the decision to meet them there. What a perfect way to repay their debt to her. She knew what kind of cars to look for all the way down to the plates on the vehicles, so imagine her surprise when she saw the BMW on the side of the road in a rainstorm with two blown-out tires. She drove right past it when the shooters she sent ahead of her called her and told her they heard screaming coming from an inn a few minutes ahead. For once Sadie seemed to be on time in the whole ordeal.

As soon as the doors were kicked down she and her shooters began to body everybody holding a sharp weapon, which was everyone in sight, until there was nobody left. The leader, a woman in a black dress, put up the toughest fight she'd ever seen in life. No matter how many bullets entered her body she still tried to reach the two sliced-up women with her machete. There was a crazed look in her eyes and Sadie swore she screamed at the girls, asking them for something . . . but she couldn't have heard what she thought she did. The woman didn't drop dead until she had ten bullets in her chest and another fifteen in other places of her body.

When Sadie's shooters turned on the two still-breathing women in the room she stopped them from firing. There was a war going on inside of the inn, and it was clear to see that they were the ones being attacked. That and the fact that they weren't dressed in slutty clothes set them apart from everyone else in the inn. When she got a good look at them women, even with cuts on their faces she knew they were the two she was looking for. Instead of murdering them in cold blood right then and there she had them transported to her home in Detroit.

"Mmm." The older of the two women stirred in her sleep. She was still cut up pretty bad but the doctor Sadie hired to nurse them back to health stitched up the gash on her neck very well. Sadie sat patiently in the chair to the side of her and waited for her eyes to open. She wore a simple yellow blouse with frills along her cleavage and a peach body con skirt. On her crossed feet she wore her yellow Chanel house shoes.

"W . . . where am I ?" the girl asked in a muzzy voice. Sadie watched her eyes open and survey the large guest room in a daze. When she realized she had tubes coming from her body, the girl panicked. Her hands rummaged over her body and felt all of the tubes there and then tried to pull them out. "Rhonnie! Rhonnie!"

"I wouldn't do that if I were you." Sadie finally extended her voice when the girl tried to sit up. "You lost a lot of blood. You're going to make yourself lightheaded."

"Madame?" The girl turned her head toward Sadie and squinted her eyes.

"Don't insult me like that." Sadie chuckled. "That crazy bitch came face to face with the best shooters in the nation. She's dead."

"But how?"

"What is your name?" Sadie asked, ignoring her question.

"Ahli."

"Well, Ahli, a few months ago you and that girl in the bed next to you did something very bad. You robbed me."

"Robbed you?"

"Yes, me. Of two hundred thousand dollars' worth of product, but you sold it for only half of that."

The comprehension of what she was being told was sinking into Ahli's mind and she inhaled a sharp breath. Brayland told her that they were savage, and looking into Sadie's eyes she knew that was true. "The Last Kings."

"Correct." Sadie rested her arm on the chair she was sitting in so that she could rest her head on her hand. "You two had me personally traveling across the world for two months looking for you. I missed out on money because of you. Give me one good reason why I shouldn't kill you both."

Ahli turned to face her sister, who looked worse than she did. Her body was completely covered in deep cuts and Ahli felt like somebody was squeezing her heart with their palm. She turned her face back to the woman and evened her breath before speaking. "What is your name?"

"I am Sadie."

"Well, Sadie, I honestly don't know why you shouldn't kill us both; but if that is what you decide to do I'm asking that you just kill me and not her. You can torture me for all eternity as long as you don't lay a finger on my sister's head. Oh, and get her some plastic surgery and shit, too. You have on Chanel slippers. You can afford it."

Sadie didn't expect to laugh but it snuck up on her and out of her mouth. She stopped it as soon as she heard it and she tried to make her expression stony again. She raised her eyebrow at the girl she'd made sure got the best medical treatment in the state, and she knew that she wasn't going to kill her. There were a few things that she needed to know.

"I figured you two were sisters," Sadie said, thinking about how the body of the younger girl, Rhonnie, was thrown over her big sister. "I just have one question."

"Yeah?"

"How did you all end up in that situation?"

"I didn't have my gun," Ahli said in all seriousness. "All of our weapons were in the room with my . . . my friend. And Madame had him killed."

"You mean Brayland?"

Ahli couldn't help but sit up in her bed at the mention of his name. "How do you know him?"

"My shooters found him assed out in one of the rooms at that whorehouse. He had been stabbed in his shoulder and chest, but he's a'ight."

"Is he here?"

Sadie smiled at Ahli, knowing the look on her face too well. It reminded her of someone she knew. "Yes. He's been in here checking on you every day when he's not training with my shooters. I actually just had to kick him out when the doctor said you were stirring in your sleep. He loves you, you know."

"I know," Ahli whispered, kicking her bare feet under the warm comforter. She cleared her throat. "Wait. Your shooters? Where are we?"

"Detroit," Sadie replied. "The headquarters of the Last Kings. I had you both relocated here. Figured you didn't have much to live for in Nebraska anymore."

Flashes of her father came to her mind but Ahli quickly pushed them away. Sadie was right, and although she didn't know what was to come she was happy to be in a new place. She swallowed and looked back at the beautiful woman with the sharp brown eyes. "I thought kings were men, not women."

"I guess I changed that rule, didn't I?" Sadie smiled at the boldness of the woman. "And if you two are who I think you are, your reputation says that you are kings too."

"Maybe, maybe not. Kings don't get caught slipping like that and almost die."

Sadie became quiet for a second and subconsciously touched the scar from the bullet that had once penetrated her chest. "You'd be surprised."

"So what now? Are you going to kill us?"

Sadie stood up from her seat and approached the bed so that she could fluff Ahli's pillows. "Not if you answer one more question for me."

"Shoot."

"How did the two of you end up in that hotel?"

"I guess . . . I guess our pasts, pasts we didn't even know about, came back to haunt us. That woman . . . that woman was looking for something in us. Something that we don't have."

"What was that woman looking for? What did she want so bad?"

Her gaze pierced Ahli's, daring her to lie, but for some odd reason Ahli didn't even want to lie. She wanted an outlet, and right then with Rhonnie still sleeping she had the perfect one.

"*Vita E Morte,*" Ahli told her.

"Life and death," Sadie whispered. "You're lying. That drug is supposed to be an Italian myth. They say the person in possession of *Vita E Morte* could do either two things: give life or cause death. Hence the name."

"Apparently not, and my mother was the one who finally got her hands on the formula to it."

"What did she do with it?" Sadie asked not in greed, but in wonder.

"She hid it," Ahli said. "She and my father didn't want it to get into the wrong hands. My father said that they destroyed it but I didn't believe him. Honestly, I don't even care about it. For me it didn't give life. It caused nothing but death around me. Rhonnie is the only family I have left in this world."

Sadie nodded her head and took a step back from the bed. "You don't have any idea where your parents would have hidden it?"

"Like I told Madame, I have no idea—"

The sight of the sun peeking through the glass window in the room caught her attention, and the sound of her mother's voice entered her head as a memory was jogged.

"Go on now. Be the good big sis I know you can be. And when we get home I'll teach you how to play Vita."

"The piano," Ahli said, looking out the window into the bright sun. She grinned and looked back to Sadie. "My mother named her piano Vita and after she died my father put it in storage. He never knew I took it out to put in my secret apartment that he obviously knew about the whole time. I could bet my life on it that the formula for *Vita E Morte* is in my mother's old piano."

"What would you say if I told you I wanted it and I need the address to your apartment?"

"I would ask you what you were going to use it for."

Sadie didn't answer right away. She just began her walk to exit the room. When she was almost to the doorway she paused and turned back around to face her.

"I would finally have the power to merge all of the major cartels together," she said softly. "The world looked at drug dealers as crooks without realizing it is our money that keeps the streets clean. The truth is harder to absorb than light. They don't want to acknowledge that it is our money, our dirty money, that they ask for to fund much-needed research practices. Yes, it is true that some of the drugs people sell poison the streets, but that is not how the Last Kings operate. I'd rather poison the people already poisoning the system. The rich sons of bitches who look down their noses at us like we're the scum. They say money is the root of all evil, but with a drug like *Vita E Morte* I'd be able to end so much death and poverty, except with the ones who wage war with us, and breathe life back into the streets. This drug has the ability to change the game and how it is played . . . forever."

There wasn't a bone in Ahli's body that didn't believe what Sadie was telling her. Her words were touching and Ahli swallowed again, trying not to cry in front of what might be the world's bossiest chick ever.

"Then I would tell you my address and tell you to grab my favorite underwear while you're at it."

Sadie grinned at her response and winked. "Rest up," Sadie told her. "Because the moment you're able to move around I'm putting you to work. All Brayland has been doing is bragging about these skills you and your sister have. I want to see them, and if they are up to par I want you to teach my men everything you know."

"What does that mean? That we can stay?"

"Yes. The loyalty your sister showed you when she threw her body over you to protect you from those blades was a special kind of love." Their eyes graced Rhonnie's sleeping body. "Shielding someone from a bullet with your body is different from shielding someone from an array of knives. She felt every bit of that pain and didn't budge off of you. She took every single last cut for you. Love like that, even between siblings, doesn't come around that often. I need that kind of loyalty and trust on my team. Plus, I must admit, it's pretty gangster that two chicks robbed a trap house full of niggas. If you accept this invitation I'd like to welcome you to the Last Kings."

Ahli thought about it for a few seconds before smirking. "It truly is crazy how things work out." Ahli briefly glanced at her sister again and felt a rush of fondness that was so strong. "But, weird as it may sound, I think we are exactly where we need to be. We don't have a family anymore, and it seems that Brayland has already made himself at home here. As long as you don't have any machetes around . . . I'm in."